A SPINSTER NO MORE

SECOND CHANCE REGENCY ROMANCE (BOOK 4)

ROSE PEARSON

D1304509

LANDON HILL MEDIA

A SPINSTER NO MORE

PROLOGUE

July 1819, London

IT WAS A PERFECTLY LOVELY WEDDING. The bride looked radiant. The groom had a smug and contented smile. But Everton Cormick was struggling to find pleasure in it. He forced himself to smile, and he dutifully danced with everyone he should. The food was excellent, which was at least something to be glad of. He congratulated the happy couple with as much enthusiasm as he could, but his heart was elsewhere.

"You are thinking of her, aren't you?" Lady Gertrude St. John said as she sidled up next to him and gave his hand a gentle squeeze. The younger sister of one of his oldest friends, Lady Gertrude was an unusual girl. Still young, barely sixteen, but very astute, she saw things many did not. There was not much anyone could hide from her.

"It is hard not to," Everton said. "We would have been wed for three years now, had she lived."

"Do you miss her so very much?"

"Every day," Everton admitted as the Master of Ceremonies called the next dance. "But now is not the time to be dwelling upon my dear Katherine." He stood up straight and smoothed down his jacket. "I believe we are to dance the *quadrille.*"

He offered Lady Gertrude his arm and she took it with a smile. It was hard to believe that this poised young woman had just survived her first Season. Beautiful, accomplished and the talk of *the Ton,* Lady Gertrude had been the belle of the Season – but to him, she would always be his dear friend, Claveston St. John, Earl of Wycliffe's little sister. She was far too observant for her own good though and seemed to have grown up almost overnight. They stepped out onto the dance floor and took their places.

Lady Gertrude grinned at her older brother as he and his new bride, Lady Sophie took their places beside them. "Wycliffe, you look positively like the cat that got the cream," Everton said to his friend, then bowed to Lady Sophie. "You look lovely, Lady Wycliffe. I only hope you will not come to regret your choice."

"You must call me Sophie," she urged, her delightful, but subtle, French accent as warm and inviting as always. "Are we not friends?"

"I believe we are," Everton agreed, "and I shall be delighted to do so."

The music started and the couples on the floor began to dance the steps, moving around the floor. "I thought, for a moment, that dear Sophie had caught your heart, Everton," Lady Gertrude said with a soft smile as she watched her brother and his new wife over Everton's shoulder. "I think Claveston did, too."

"She is very lovely," Everton admitted. "But..."

"You still don't see anyone that way?" Lady Gertrude said gently.

"No, and I doubt if I ever will."

"That is sad, and I doubt what Lady Katherine would have wanted for you. She always seemed to be so full of life and living - but I did not know her all that well."

They finished their dance. Everton bowed politely as Lady Gertrude dipped him a curtsey. "Do you have any dances free?" she asked him as he escorted her from the dance floor.

"I think so," he said. "Well, I have one. The waltz."

"Oh, I am so glad," she said as she led him towards a very pretty looking young lady with dark ringlets, ruddy cheeks and bright blue eyes who had been standing in the corner of the ballroom, looking nervous, throughout the entire evening. Lady Gertrude beamed at her. "This is Miss Anne Knorr," she said nodding towards the petite young lady. "I'm not sure if you were introduced at Lord William and Lady Mary's nuptials, but Miss Knorr was Mary's companion, before they were married."

"Delighted to make your acquaintance, Miss Knorr," Everton said as he gave her a deep bow. "Everton Cormick, at your service." She flushed prettily, her rosy cheeks glowing an ever-brighter shade of red. She dipped her head as she curtseyed, keeping her eyes down as if to hide it, which Everton found rather sweet.

"Honored," Miss Knorr whispered.

"Should you like to dance?" he asked her as the Master of Ceremonies called everyone to the floor for the waltz. She glanced nervously at Lady Gertrude before nodding. He offered her his hand. She placed hers over his and he led her onto the floor.

The waltz was an intimate dance. It had been decried by many as lascivious and licentious but had grown popular despite its reputation – or perhaps, because of it. Everton placed his hand in the center of Miss Knorr's back and smiled as she rested her hand upon his shoulder. The music started and he stepped forwards. She followed his lead perfectly, her steps light and graceful. But neither of them said a word as they whirled around the floor, just one couple among many.

He escorted her back to Lady Gertrude's side once the dance was done and took his leave of the pair. There was a game of cards underway in the library, and Everton was tired of dancing. He took a seat at the card table and was dealt into the next hand. The stakes weren't high, it was a wedding after all, but enough to make the game interesting. Everton stayed in the game until the end of the evening, sometimes winning a hand, sometimes losing – but he never let himself get in too deep that he couldn't pay his debts on the night.

His old friend Captain James Watts sat across the table from him, Lord William Pierce, Earl of Cott to his right. It was good to be with them, and the conversation flowed as freely as it ever did. From time to time, they looked up and into the ballroom, where the fourth member of their quartet was forced to dance throughout the night with his bride, his sister and other members of his family, and grinned as Wycliffe mugged behind his unwanted partner's backs and gave him teasing looks as he lost himself in his wife's embrace.

"Who'd've thought it," James said shaking his head as they watched the happy couple. "Claveston St. John, the biggest cad amongst us all, settled and devoted." James had a large scar over his face from his time in the army. For a time, it had seen him shun all society – including that of his now wife, William's sister, Charlotte. Thankfully for them both, it seemed that she had convinced him that those who truly cared would always see him for the man he was. It was good to have him there.

"I know we all thought it impossible," William added. "But to tell you the truth, I always expected Cormick here to be wed before all of us, he was ever the most loyal of us and the most romantic. And here we are, all of us settled as he continues to remain free."

Everton had to disguise a grimace, as he heard the words. He knew William meant well, that he was only teasing. But it hurt that his friend could have forgotten Katherine so easily – and how much her death from influenza, just three weeks before their planned wedding three years ago, had broken Everton into pieces. But as he looked at William's face, he could see that he regretted his words as soon as he'd uttered them. "I'm sorry, old friend, he said softly. "I spoke out of turn."

"No, you did not," Everton assured him. "You meant nothing by it. It is true enough, that had things gone the way I had planned them, I would have been wed long before all of you – though it turned out that all of you were hot upon my heels. It has been quite the few years for us all."

They all nodded their agreement at that. "So, who is prepared to make a little wager on how long it will be before there is an heir to the St. John name?" Everton said doing all he could to change the subject and move it away from himself and the loss of the woman he continued to mourn.

"I doubt it will be long," William said, warming to the wager. "I'll guess within a year, and stake fifty pounds."

"I'd give them no more than 10 months," James said. "I know Sophie well. She and Charlotte are as close as sisters. I know how much she longs for a child."

"Which gives me little to work with, my friends," Everton joked. "But I shall say within eighteen months. We shall all have to watch to see which of us is right." The three men shook upon their wager and returned to their card game. They had been friends since school, and he could not imagine better men to have by his side. Even Wycliffe, though he had seemed to blow easily in the wind until he met his bride, would have done all in his power to support any one of them. It was a pleasure to be able to share their happiness with them, though he also couldn't help feeling a little envious of them.

"When do you leave us?" Lady Gertrude St. John asked as they sipped at their cups of fruit punch.

"Tomorrow," Anne replied, dabbing at her lips as she set down her now empty cup.

Lady Gertrude tucked an arm through Anne's. "I cannot tell you how jealous I am of Caroline Spencer, that you are to be her companion. If I had known that I would be looking for a new one myself at the end of this Season, I should have tried to snaffle you up."

Anne smiled. "I did not know until very recently of Lady Jacinda Ardern's engagement; she kept it quiet from everyone, even me. I did not know that I would be moving on again myself until just a few days ago. It was Lady Jacinda that found me the position with Miss Spencer who is the daughter of one of her Mama's dearest friends. I shall go to the family seat in Northumberland and spend the coming months there with her, preparing her for her first Season."

"And here I am, companionless," Lady Gertrude said dramatically. "Can you not change your mind? Oh, do say you will, and will come back to Compton with me? Northumberland is so terribly far away, and I shall be so terribly lonely with Claveston and Sophie away in France for their wedding tour."

Anne laughed. She knew that Lady Gertrude was just being kind. The two of them had little in common, but she feared she had even less in common with Miss Caroline Spencer, who was as outgoing and vivacious as Anne was quiet and reserved. A position in the St. John household would possibly have suited her better, but she was not in a position to be choosy. She did not doubt that the Duke and Duchess of Compton would be looking for a companion for Lady Gertrude of the highest caliber and breeding. Anne Knorr, though her father was a minor baronet, could not claim such attributes.

She was saved from answering though, by the arrival of a young captain, who clicked his heels and bowed sharply, offering Lady Gertrude his hand, and escorting her to the dancefloor. Anne smiled then ducked out of the ballroom. She snuck outside onto the terrace for some peace and quiet. To think that she had begged her father to let her leave Tulilly, so she might experience some excitement. She had barely been gone a few years and was already sick of London and the social whirl that being in Society entailed.

She wished that the Lady Mary had been able to attend this evening. Being her companion had been easy. Lady Mary was as quiet and bookish as Anne herself was, though she was more than capable of acting well in Society. But Lady Mary was heavy with child and had remained in the countryside, in her beloved Alnerton, for the sake of her and her unborn baby's health. Yet Anne was flattered to have been invited to Lady Sophie and Lord Wycliffe's nuptials. It was an invitation she had not expected, though she had come to know Lady Sophie well during her time in Alnerton with Lady Mary.

Footsteps behind her made Anne turn abruptly. The gentleman who had been kind enough to ask her to dance stood by the French doors, looking a little sheepish. "I'm sorry," he said awkwardly. "I should go back inside. I didn't know anyone was out here."

"You needn't," Anne said. "I just wished for a little air."

"Me, too," Mr. Cormick said with a wry smile. "I'm not always too keen on merriment at weddings."

"You don't believe in marriage? In love?" His comment surprised Anne. He had seemed to be very much involved in the events of the day, and always had a beaming smile for everyone. She'd watched him dance with many of the young woman present, making each and every one of them feel special. She had seen it in the way their eyes lit up when they were around him.

"Oh, I believe in them alright," he said. "Just for everyone else."

"Not for yourself?"

"No," he said, narrowing his eyes a little and taking a step closer. "It's Miss Knorr, is it not?" Anne nodded. "We danced a waltz earlier, I believe."

"Yes, Mr. Cormick, we did," she said. It had been one of the highlights of her evening. So few people ever noticed her – which made her an excellent companion, but was a little hard on her. It often made her feel invisible, unwanted – and unloved.

"You are a very fine dancer," he told her solemnly. "Quite the best I have had the pleasure of partnering in many years. Thank you."

"Thank you," Anne said, flushing puce at his compliment. "I... I doubt I am any better than anyone else, but I practice hard." She paused and looked around. There was nobody there to see them, but somehow being out here alone, in the dark, with a handsome man seemed to be very wrong indeed. Her position existed to ensure her charges never found themselves in such a predicament – one that could ruin a girl's reputation in a heartbeat – and yet, here she was herself. "I should go back inside before I am missed," she added awkwardly. "Thank you again, for the dance."

"It was my pleasure," he said, as he watched her dart towards the door. She tried to keep her distance from him, but he was right there, and as she went for the door, it meant she had to brush past him. She looked up at him, her eyes wide. He looked down at her and for a moment, their eyes held, as if they recognized something in one another. Anne felt as though she had gooseflesh all over her body, yet no bumps were raised upon her skin while every inch of her tingled. She wanted to pull away, knew she should pull away, yet she could not. His blue eyes were deep, like the ocean, and she felt as though she were lost in them.

But the moment passed as quickly as it had come. Mr. Cormick stepped out of her way. Anne shook her head almost imperceptibly and turned the door handle. She hurried inside and into the ballroom, where she could hide amongst the happy revelers, who never seemed to notice her much anyway. But that moment played on her mind, far too much in the weeks to come.

CHAPTER ONE

F*ebruary 1820, London*

THE ENTRANCE HALL of Almack's was thronged with
giggling girls, all shrieking with delight as they encoun-
tered their friends and relations at the first Wednesday
night ball of the Season. Anne untied the ribbon of her
cape and took it off, handing it to the footman and
watched as her new charge, Miss Caroline Spencer did
the same. She glanced around, seeing a few familiar faces,
but nobody she might call a real friend. She sighed heavily, dreading the months of such events as this one ahead
of her.

Why did every young woman come to London so full
of excitement? Anne shook her head as she watched the
glowing faces all around her. They'd soon lose that
enthusiasm when they realized that they would have to
spend the next few months surrounded by the very same

people, doing the very same things, over and over again, in the vain hope that some man might notice them – preferably young, rich and titled, but that he be of good breeding was paramount. It rarely took long for the endless round of balls and soirees, luncheons and musicales to wear on the nerves if no such match seemed forthcoming.

Anne watched the young women of *the Ton* as they gathered for this evening's entertainments. This, the first of Almack's Wednesday night balls, was one of the first events of the Season. All the eligible young women present fluttered around like giddy butterflies, all eager to show off their new gowns and to catch up on gossip they might have missed. They seemed even younger and sillier than ever this Season. Anne wondered if that was because she was getting older, or if it was because she simply didn't want to be here anymore. She would gladly return to Tulilly or Alnerton tomorrow if she could.

And this year things were to be even more extravagant than ever. Following the death of his father, the Prince Regent would have his coronation towards the end of the Season and would finally become King in name as well as duties. By all accounts it was to be a lavish affair and everyone in town wished to be invited. He was older now, fat - and apparently prone to rather unpleasant moods. There were even rumors that he had a tendency to use a little too much laudanum. As the Prince Regent, he had been self-indulgent, spoiled and extravagant – but he had also been a patron of the arts and had been considered charming by many. Anne was not sure if he would make a good king, but the spectacle of his coronation would at least be something to make this Season stand out from all the others.

Her new charge, Miss Spencer, was no different to every other giddy sixteen-year-old in London for the first time. She had been the toast of the county in Northumberland and expected to be no less in the capital. She was pretty, with blonde hair that curled becomingly and wide blue eyes that made her seem innocent and sweet. She was neither partridge plump or too thin and had an income of fifteen thousand pounds per year. She could dance beautifully, paint exquisite watercolors, and sang like a lark. Yet underneath her beauty, she was calculating and determined. She knew what she wanted, and that was to marry well – and to do it fast so she might never have to return to Northumberland again. She did not yet realize that her choice of husband might offer her even less happiness than her current situation – despite all of Anne's warnings to that effect.

Following Anne's arrival in Northumberland, it had not taken the two young women long to learn that they had little in common. Anne did not much like her new charge and often wished that she had been able to become Lady Gertrude St. John's companion instead. But that position had not been offered to her by the Duke and Duchess of Compton, Gertrude's parents – and even if it had been, it would have been too late. She had already accepted the offer from Mr. Spencer, a wealthy industrialist who was determined that his daughter might marry a duke, or at least an earl, in order to make his grandchildren respectable to *the Ton* in a way he knew he never would be.

The girls scurried around, determined to fill their dance cards without seeming to be doing so. With each new partner, a quick gloat amongst one's friends seemed to be essential, so the introductions and pleasantries took much longer than they truly needed to. As Anne watched, the more ridiculous the entire thing seemed to her. To her, the clamoring seemed no different to that at the Exeter cattle market, where farmers fought over the finest beasts. The Season was a market just the same, where wealthy and titled men came to choose a well-mannered and wealthy wife. If she was pretty and titled, too, then so much the better. The girls were often too young and too romantic to realize the true nature of their presence here.

It was clear that Miss Spencer's arrival in London had caused quite a stir, as was so often the case with a pretty and accomplished new face. Anne cynically wondered if it was because of her charge's beauty that Miss Spencer was so sought out, or her fifteen thousand a year. Perhaps it might be both – but it certainly wasn't for her sweet nature, because Miss Spencer did not possess such a thing. She was selfish, vain and utterly uninterested in anything that did not pertain to her own happiness.

Yet despite that, Miss Spencer's dance card was filled in no time with a number of prominent names, including the most sought-after bachelors in London this Season. Miss Spencer wasted no time in gloating about it. "Try and be a little more gracious," Anne whispered in her ear. "Your companions will not like you if you lord it over them – and your suitors will look elsewhere if they think you are not kind."

Miss Spencer nodded politely and raised her opened fan to her face. "You are my companion, not my tutor," she hissed spitefully.

"I am indeed only your companion," Anne agreed quietly. "But you told me you wished for my guidance and to tell you if you were not doing things as you should be. I have escorted two young women before you and seen what it takes to win a husband. You must be sweet and generous, kind and gentle, Miss Spencer. No man wishes to wed a shrew."

The young girl looked decidedly put out, but Anne knew that she would take the lesson to heart. Miss Spencer wished to be married too badly to ignore good advice – and Anne wished to be free to go home. Mrs. Spencer had already told her daughter often enough that she would have to pretend to be something she was not. And Miss Spencer was an excellent actress. "Stop frowning, you don't want lines," Anne added as Miss Spencer pinned a smile to her lovely face and lowered her fan as if nothing untoward had been said.

She took Miss Spencer's card and ran a finger down the names signed up for each dance. She gave her charge a brief description of those she knew and the things they liked. Miss Spencer nodded, and Anne knew she was memorizing every word. She would use the information to make polite conversation as they danced and would try to make a good impression. Anne had no doubt that there would be a number of calling cards delivered to the Mayfair townhouse in the morning and that Miss

Spencer would have her pick of who to take her into supper and escort her home.

Mrs. Spencer had spent a number of hours impressing upon Anne how important it would be that Miss Spencer was never left alone with any young man for too long, to ensure he did not see signs of the girl's true nature before becoming besotted enough to ask for her hand. While Anne could feel sorry for any child whose parents seemed to have such a low opinion of their offspring, it was easy to see why. Miss Spencer had grown up believing that she was better than most people – and that she deserved much more than she already possessed. Yet such beliefs had to have come from somewhere, and Anne was sure it was her parents' mistakes that had led to it. They had spoiled her terribly.

As Miss Spencer began her evening, dancing every dance, Anne moved into a quiet corner. She was not much impressed by balls and dances. She didn't mind card parties and music evenings, but the supposed glamor of the Season had lost its charm very quickly after her arrival from Exeter to accompany Lady Mary as she navigated her first Season. She'd much rather be at home with a good book. And that was exactly where she intended to go, as soon as she had seen Miss Caroline Spencer affianced and wed.

As the evening passed, she kept her eyes on Miss Spencer the entire time. It would not do to have her charge make an error in her first few days in London. The Season was long and there were many hurdles to be crossed. A mistake would be held against her for the rest of her life and would mean that Anne would not be released from Miss Spencer's service for many years to come.

"It is you," a familiar voice declared nearby. Anne looked up to see the smiling face of Lady Gertrude St. John and her new companion as they approached. "Dear Miss Knorr, how are you?"

"I am well, Lady Gertrude," Anne said smiling back at them both. Lady Gertrude looked lovely, as always. Her companion was older, perhaps in her late twenties, and had a bright smile and a light step.

"This is Eleanor Jessup," Lady Gertrude said, pushing her companion forward. "She is my new Sophie."

"Delighted to meet you. Everyone speaks very highly of you," Miss Jessup said, clearly not at all put out to be called Gertrude's new Sophie.

"Have you had word from your brother and Lady Sophie?" Anne asked. "I understood that they had extended their trip because they were enjoying the sights of Europe so much."

"I think Sophie just does not wish to leave her family," Lady Gertrude said with a warm smile as she thought about her brother and new sister-in-law. "But they assure me that they are to do one further trip, to Rome this time, and that they will return in time for the King's coronation."

"And have you yet met Mary's baby?" Anne asked eagerly. She had been unable to get away from Northumberland when the child was born and had been sad to have to turn down Mary and Lord William's invitation to the child's baptism in October.

"I have. I attended the baptism and stood as Claveston's proxy as they chose him to be godfather to little Nathaniel. Mary and William chose Captain Watts and Charlotte as his other godparents."

"Was it a wonderful celebration?"

"It was. Lady Mary and Lord William looked so unbelievably happy, and Nathaniel is a lusty boy, with a fine appetite."

"I am glad. I so wished to attend."

"I know your presence was missed, though everyone understood why you could not get away. They were very touched by the gifts you sent in your stead."

"Mary wrote me a lovely letter, thanking me," Anne said. "It was the very least I could do."

"Then I presume she told you that they are expecting another child?" Lady Gertrude said excitedly. "She must have already been *enceinte* at the baptism itself."

"She did, and it is wonderful news," Anne agreed. She had been able to tell just how delighted Mary had been about it in her most recent letter. She had waxed most poetic about the pleasures of pregnancy and motherhood, gifts she had assumed that would never be hers.

Lady Gertrude glanced around the room, as if looking for someone very specific. She tutted and tapped her foot a little, then looked back at Anne. "Did you know, Everton Cormick and his brother are in town," she said, a tone of exasperation in her voice. "They promised they would be here tonight, but I've not seen them. It would be just like them to get here late once every girls' dance card is filled so they can leave immediately after supper to go to their club and play cards."

"Mr. Cormick?" Anne said, trying to sound nonchalant. She still recalled that moment on the terrace, and how it had felt to be in his arms as they'd waltzed at Lady Sophie's wedding.

"Yes, they are doing some work for their father, who has had to remain in Hertfordshire. A minor health scare I'm told, so the brothers are in charge of everything for a while. Mr. Cormick assured me he would be here to act as my big brother in Claveston's place – to help me weed out the suitors not worthy of my attentions."

"I am sure Mr. Cormick will do a fine job of that," Anne said, her heart suddenly beating a little faster and harder than usual. "I am sure if he promised he would be here, that he will arrive in good time for supper." Anne bit at her lip. She should not be surprised that he was in town. She knew that the family were very successful merchants and that both sons had followed their father into his enterprise. She would have to do all she could not to get her hopes up that he might notice her once more, and perhaps even dance with her again.

CHAPTER TWO

"I don't want to go," Henry said, pouting as he tousled his unruly dark curls and reluctantly let Everton help him into his emerald velvet evening jacket. "Why can't I just go to the club?"

"Because Mama wants you to find a wife – and you promised you would at least try," Everton said firmly, giving his brother a shove out of the door, down the stairs and outside the house. The carriage was waiting, a footman holding open the door.

"Why do you not have to find a wife? You're older than me – and much better suited to married life. You actually like talking to girls."

"Henry, you are old enough to have gotten past such nonsense," Everton scolded. "And Mama does not nag me to find a wife because I already did." He gave his brother a cold stare as he tried to keep his temper under control. It was hurtful that Henry would say such a thing, knowing how badly hurt Everton had been in the past.

Henry did at least have the decency to look contrite.

"I'm sorry," he said grumpily as Everton pushed him down the stairs onto the street and waited for his brother to get into the carriage.

"Can I at least go after supper?" Henry sulked as he got in and shifted across the bench to the other side so Everton could follow behind him.

"We'll barely arrive before supper at this rate," Everton said testily.

"That's no loss," Henry said. "Everyone knows that the food at Almack's is inedible."

"Do not let any of the Lady Patronesses hear you say such a thing," Everton said, but couldn't stop himself from grinning. It was true enough, the food was rarely enjoyable – but Almack's was the most important ticket in town, and they were lucky enough to receive the vouchers needed to attend – given they had no titles between them.

"Sometimes I wish Mama wasn't the daughter of an earl," Henry grumbled. "If only she hadn't been friends with Countess Lieven."

"Well, she is, and so we must do our best not to let her down." Everton sighed heavily. "There are many young men that would be delighted to have a connection to one of the Lady Patronesses. They can smooth your way through Society, they are very powerful in their own way."

"I do not want my way smoothed. I do not wish to be invited to every important event. I just want to be left alone, to go to my club and to keep to my studies."

"Then find a wife quickly, one who won't mind being kept at home with nothing to do while you waste your life in a library or at a card table," Everton retorted.

The journey to Almack's was thankfully brief, and the two young men arrived half an hour before the supper gong would sound. They handed over their outer coats at the door and made their way into the ballroom. Henry winced at the level of noise but did his best to look interested in what was going on around them. Everton peered over the heads, scanning the crowd for anyone he knew. His eyes rested upon Lady Gertrude St. John. She turned and saw him, gave him a mock glare and pointed towards the clock on the wall. He grinned and grabbing his brother by the arm made his way through the crowds to where she was standing.

The brothers bowed to Lady Gertrude. "Good evening," she said drily. "I was beginning to fear you wouldn't be here, after all."

"I promised you and your brother that I would escort you around town until he could return. I am sorry for our tardiness," Everton said honestly, nudging his brother, hoping he would make his apologies too.

"It was my fault," Henry said, honestly. "I am sorry, Lady Gertrude. I do hope you will forgive me."

"I may," she said, pursing her lips, but then she smiled brightly, nudging forward her companions. "You remember Miss Knorr, do you not? From Claveston and Sophie's wedding?"

"I do," Everton said, smiling at Miss Knorr and bowing politely. "I am glad to see you again, Miss Knorr. I do hope you are well, and that your new position suits you."

"I am well," Miss Knorr said, seeming to ignore the second part of his question. "My charge, Miss Spencer is on the dance floor." She pointed out a strikingly lovely girl, who bore a striking resemblance to his lost Katherine. It shook him.

Lady Gertrude must have seen his visceral and unexpected reaction to the sight of Miss Spencer, grabbing his arm and dragging his attention back to the three women stood before him. "And this is my new companion, Miss Eleanor Jessup."

"Charmed," he said, forcing a smile. "Might I introduce my younger brother, Henry," he added. "I'm not sure you've had the pleasure, Lady Gertrude."

"No, though I have heard a lot about you from dear Mr. Cormick. It is a pleasure to finally make your acquaintance," Lady Gertrude said, a perfect model of decorum.

The supper bell rang, and Everton offered his arm to Lady Gertrude, flicking his head towards Miss Knorr and Miss Jessup in the hope that his brother might think to escort one of them into the dining room. Thankfully he did, holding out his arm for Miss Knorr, who quickly glanced over to see her charge being escorted by Captain Arthur Kingsley. "He's a good man," Everton said. "I can vouch for his honor. If we hurry though, we can catch them and sit with them at the table."

Miss Knorr smiled gratefully at him. "Thank you. I am conscious that it is my job to ensure she remains safe. I should so hate for her to choose the wrong sort, right from the start."

"Kingsley wouldn't hurt a fly. One of the most gallant men I know," he assured her.

Everton subtly elbowed his way through the crowds so that they entered the dining room just behind Miss Spencer. He couldn't help marveling at how like his lost Katherine the girl was. He wanted to reach out and touch her blonde ringlets, to see if they were as soft as Katherine's had been. It took everything he had not to call out his lost fiancée's name to see if she would turn around.

Soon they were all seated and additional introductions had been made. Conversation was soon lively. He smiled to see his brother actually talking with Miss Knorr quite animatedly. He wondered what subject had caught his brother's attention sufficiently for him to be so involved. He thought about how sweet and quiet Miss Knorr was and wondered if perhaps she might be just the kind of woman that would suit Henry best. At least he would now have someone other than himself that Henry was disposed to converse with to tempt his brother out into Society more often.

As the meal drew to a close, any illusions he might have possessed about Miss Spencer being a reincarnation of his lost love had been smashed. Where Katherine had been sweet, Miss Spencer was cold. Katherine's generosity of spirit and warmth of heart was utterly missing in Miss Spencer. All she talked about was herself and her own accomplishments. She didn't show even the tiniest interest in those around her. Not surprisingly, Captain Kingsley soon turned to talk with Miss Jessup who was seated to his right, where Miss Spencer had been to his left. This left the young woman at the very edge of their little group, pouting at being left out of the conversation. Though it didn't take long for the young man seated to her left to see that his chance had come. Miss Spencer's smile was immediately back in place and she began charming the silly fool who didn't care one bit about what she said, as long as she said it to him.

Everton couldn't help feeling sorry for Miss Knorr that she had to accompany such an unpleasant young woman to all the events of what would be one of the busiest Seasons in many years. He turned to see her watching her charge. He gave her what he hoped would be interpreted as a supportive look. She rolled her eyes and shrugged. It was obvious she knew just who she was chaperoning and what to expect from her.

The rest of the evening passed in good temper. Miss Spencer danced every dance, so they did not have to entertain her. Lady Gertrude danced from time to time but seemed little inclined to dance with anyone unless she already liked them. Everton asked Miss Jessup to dance, which prompted his brother to ask Miss Knorr to make up a four. As they danced, Everton was reminded again of what an excellent dancer Miss Knorr was. She seemed to really feel both the music and the steps and enjoyed herself as she did so. She smiled, and it lit up her face. He hadn't realized until that moment how rarely she seemed to smile, and how lovely she was when she did.

As the evening drew to a close, he offered to see Lady Gertrude and Miss Jessup home. Henry stood by awkwardly, but didn't offer the same to Miss Knorr, but Lord Haworth Westley had already offered to see Miss Spencer home, so as her companion Miss Knorr would have been unable to accept, anyway. Everton watched as the incongruous trio of the stunningly lovely looking, but haughty and unpleasant Miss Spencer with her aging and heavily jowled suitor who might as well have been drooling he was so transparent about his desire for her, and the quiet and demure Miss Knorr made their way into the cool spring night. He shook his head, then offered Lady Gertrude his arm.

As they went outside, Henry pulled him to one side. "D'you mind if I just go straight to my club?" he asked. "You don't need me, for this, do you?"

Now it was Everton's time to roll his eyes. "If you must. Don't lose your entire allowance at once," he warned him, then sighed heavily as Henry almost ran down the street away from them.

"I see he is still not reformed," Lady Gertrude said as Everton turned to help her into her carriage, then Miss Jessup.

"No," Everton said getting inside and sitting opposite them, tapping the roof with his cane to tell the driver to move on. "He is young, thinks Father will always get him out of a tight spot, and that he need never change."

"Perhaps your father should stop adding to his allowance each time he loses."

"I've suggested that, but Henry is so rarely happy about anything, I think my father fears if he doesn't indulge him that Henry will fall into a pit of melancholy."

"Perhaps it is the gambling that makes him melancholy. If he could give it up, then he may be happier," Miss Jessup suggested tentatively. "It is not my place to say, but my father had the same problem." Everton nodded. He feared much the same. But getting Henry away from his club long enough to break his habit would not be easy.

"He seemed quite taken with Miss Knorr," Lady Gertrude noted. "Perhaps that is something that might jolt him out of it, the love of a good woman?"

"D'you know, I was thinking the same thing myself," Everton admitted. "D'you think we might find ways in which to throw them together? I think they'd make an excellent match."

"I think we can ensure they attend enough of the same events. They are both quiet and prefer the company of those they know. They will likely enough gravitate towards one another. I shall make a point of making Miss Spencer my dearest friend this Season – though let it be known, I do this for you, Mr. Cormick for all you mean to my brother."

Everton smiled wryly. "Yes, she is rather a dragon, is she not," he said. "Poor Miss Knorr, to have to live day in and day out with such a piece of work."

CHAPTER THREE

A *pril, 1820, London*

THERE WAS one thing to be said of the London Season, there was little time to stop and think. Anne, the companion of one of the most beautiful young debutantes in town that year, found her days and nights filled with a whirl of activities. Within just the first month, she and Miss Spencer had attended the theatre, the ballet and the symphony. They had taken tea in six, no seven homes more than once since their arrival, and had attended three card parties, four supper parties, and eight musicales - as well as the weekly ball at Almack's. When they weren't busy with all of that, Miss Spencer insisted on ordering the carriage every day in order to take a drive through the park, or to promenade if the weather was fine.

A number of young men seemed quite smitten, and

Miss Spencer was doing her best to hide her more unpleasant nature. Every morning brought a silver salver with a number of gentlemen's cards upon it, wishing to call upon her or to attend the Spencers' At Home, which was held on a Thursday afternoon. Each week, after lunch, Anne helped Miss Spencer into her prettiest gowns as her maid curled her hair and then the two young women sat in the parlor, praying someone might come.

"Do you think Lord Wilson will come?" Miss Spencer said agitatedly, getting up from her chair and moving to the window to peer out onto the street.

"Come away," her mother scolded. "Sit patiently. He assured your father he would call upon us and he does not seem to be the kind of man that would break a promise to me." Mrs. Spencer had the burr of a northern accent, though her daughter had done all she could to eradicate her own. Whenever her mother spoke, Miss Spencer winced as if embarrassed.

"Just try not to talk too much if anyone deigns to wait upon me today," Miss Spencer said. Her tone wasn't malicious, but it made her mother duck her head as if trying to hide her feelings of shame. Anne often wondered if Miss Spencer was even aware that her bluntness could be so hurtful – she certainly showed little sign of it.

"I shall be silent as the grave," Mrs. Spencer said, folding her hands in her lap and biting at her lip.

A knock at the door had Miss Spencer jumping to her feet and trying to see who had arrived. She frowned. "It is only Lady Gertrude and Miss Jessup," she said and sank down onto one of the elegant couches, slouching grumpily.

"You should be grateful of her friendship," Mrs. Spencer said. "Lady St. John is from a fine family, and she knows all the best people. That she has shown an interest in you is most kind of her."

Miss Spencer rolled her eyes but jumped to her feet and curtseyed deeply when Lady Gertrude and Miss Jessup entered the room. "How kind of you to come to our little At Home, Lady Gertrude," she simpered.

"It is our pleasure, is it not Miss Jessup?" Lady Gertrude said, she gave Anne a friendly wink while Miss Spencer rose from her curtsey. "And how lovely to see you, too, Mrs. Spencer, and dear Miss Knorr." Lady Gertrude's warmth and kindness put even the anxious Mrs. Spencer at ease and soon the ladies were enjoying polite chit-chat as they were served the delicious afternoon tea laid out on the counter by the hovering parlor maids.

"Did I hear rightly, that Lord Wilson took you into supper at Lady Halstead's card party yesterday evening?" Lady Gertrude asked Miss Spencer, feigning interest.

"He did," Miss Spencer said. "He is very handsome, is he not?"

"He is that," Mrs. Spencer agreed.

"And his twenty thousand pounds a year is certainly not to be sniffed at," Lady Gertrude said cheekily. She knew all too well why all the young women of *the Ton* were hoping to catch Lord Willson's slightly squinty eyes. He was a decent enough fellow, though a little dull. Anne was sure that he was not the kind of man that Lady Gertrude would ever set her cap at.

"I had not realized his fortune so great," Miss Spencer lied. Anne had to stifle a chuckle. The young woman refused to even dance with a man now unless he had an income of at least ten thousand pounds a year and owned a London townhouse and a country estate. She cared little for a man's personality, as long as he could provide her with the escape she so desired.

"He would make a fine husband, though I heard that he was seen walking in the park earlier today with Miss Hetty Winthorpe," Lady Gertrude said, innocently enough, but from the sparkle in her eye it was clear that she was doing her best to tease Miss Spencer, whose lips were now squeezed in a tight line, her color high as she tried not to show her displeasure. "They seemed quite engrossed in one another. But I am sure it was not what it seemed."

They were saved from what might have come from Miss Spencer's angry lips by another knock at the door. "I wonder who that might be?" Lady Gertrude said, then took a sip of tea and another bite of cake, as though she didn't really care at all.

Anne wondered how Lady Gertrude managed to be so calm and so amused by Miss Spencer. She was grateful indeed, to the young woman, for befriending her young charge, but she did not understand why. Lady Gertrude had more than enough friends in Society. Her connections firmly placed her amongst the highest echelons of *the* Ton. Anne had to admit that Lady Gertrude seemed to enjoy teasing Miss Spencer, though she was not ever cruel. Anne's charge did not always appreciate Lady Gertrude's sharp wit and canny observations – but, thankfully, Miss Spencer was venal enough to see the benefit of the connection – even though it was clear that neither young woman liked the other particularly. After all, Lady Gertrude's presence guaranteed some of the finest members of *the Ton* courted Miss Spencer and sought her company, and that was not to be disregarded.

"Mr. Everton Cormick, and Henry Cormick," the butler announced as the two brothers appeared in the doorway to the parlor. Mr. Cormick was beaming, as he almost always did. Anne found him to be a very amiable man. Henry looked his usual, slightly disheveled self and fidgeted awkwardly with his cravat, as if it were tied too tight. The two gentlemen bowed and greeted the ladies present. Miss Spencer poured them both tea and prepared plates of tiny sandwiches and cakes for them both, as they took their seats upon the couch opposite Lady Gertrude.

"I cannot tell you how delighted I am to see you both," Lady Gertrude said. "We were just talking of an old friend of yours, Lord Wilson."

"Ah, Bertie," Henry said with a grin. "He's a capital fellow. Went to Oxford with him. Not much of a scholar, but loyal as they come."

"Didn't he get sent down?" Mr. Cormick asked his brother with a grin. "Something about a prank involving a cockerel and a can of paint?" Miss Spencer looked unfazed by the mention of the man being sent down from university for a prank, though her mother looked scandalized.

"It was harmless enough," Henry said, reassuringly to Mrs. Spencer. "He was egged on by some of the older chaps and he so wanted to prove himself. But he wasn't meant for the academic life. He's happier running his estates."

Within another half an hour a further seven people had come to call. The afternoon was a success. Miss Spencer's At Home had attracted some of the finest members of Society, including Lord Wilson, who seemed to have forgotten all about Miss Winthorpe. He hung on Miss Spencer's every word like a besotted puppy and so his arrival improved Miss Spencer's mood immeasurably.

This meant that Anne was free to talk with Lady Gertrude and Miss Jessup. "How does her hunt go?" Lady Gertrude asked quietly, looking towards the fireplace where Miss Spencer, Lord Wilson and Henry Cormick stood chatting.

"I think she may be in luck," Anne said, rolling her eyes. "He's just foolish enough not to notice she's not much more than a pretty face."

"I think you may be right," Lady Gertrude said seriously. "He's doing what he can to ensure that his name is not only associated with hers, but it is all too clear how devoted he is to her. I've seen him with Lady Honoria Blackwood, and dear little Hetty, but he doesn't look on them as he does Miss Spencer."

"I hope it remains so," Anne said.

"What would become of you, if your charge were to marry early in the Season?" Miss Jessup asked curiously. It was clear it was a question that concerned her. Lady Gertrude was much sought after, her position would be at risk if her charge found a husband before the Season was done.

"I do not know," Anne admitted. "But I doubt that I would be kept on. We are not close, as I was with Lady Mary, or Lady Sophie was with Lady Charlotte and Lady Gertrude." She avoided remarking upon Miss Jessup's situation, but Lady Gertrude was not so reticent.

"You need not fear for the same future," she said squeezing her companion's hand. "I have no intention of being wed this Season. I am still too young, and there is nobody here so far capable of swaying my resolve."

Miss Jessup beamed. "I am glad," she said. "Not that I do not wish you to find a husband, of course I do, but I rather enjoy my position as your companion and would hate to have to leave your service so soon." Lady Gertrude smiled, too. Anne couldn't help being a little envious of the bond that the pair shared. They had been together for a similar amount of time as she and Miss Spencer, but their friendship had blossomed. Even though they were in a room filled with people, Anne suddenly felt very alone.

Mr. Cormick approached them, having spent the last few minutes speaking with Lord Alistair Crowley, heir to the Marquess of Hartington. "Might I interrupt you?" he asked politely.

Lady Gertrude grinned at him and indicated he should take a nearby chair. "Of course, you may. How are your dear parents?"

"They are well," he said with a smile. "I received a letter from your brother, he says he and Lady Sophie will be returning within the month, should the tides permit."

"Indeed. I cannot tell you how glad I will be to see them. They have been gone far too long," Lady Gertrude said. "They intend to spend some time in London before returning to Compton, so hopefully we will all be reunited soon."

He beckoned his brother over. Henry ruffled his hair as he sank down onto the couch next to Anne. He smiled at her shyly. "It is good to see you, Miss Knorr. I have been thinking of our conversation at Almack's the other week. You said that you had been reading Miss Shelley's Frankenstein and had found it fascinating."

"I did, it made me think on things in a completely different way."

"I just read The Vampyre, by Polidori. It is an unusual book, to be sure, but I think you might like it. I can lend it to you if you would like?"

"I should, that is most kind of you, Mr. Cormick," Anne said politely. She had expected him to perhaps deliver it another day, but instead he pulled out a battered looking copy from inside his jacket.

"I never go anywhere without something good to read," he said a little shyly. "I do not always do well with people, so having something to occupy me is essential. My tailor hates that I always request a pocket in my jackets large enough."

"I am the same," Anne admitted. "Though my seam-stress would be aghast if I asked for such a thing. I do feel that books are far more easy to read than real life people, don't you think?"

They smiled together, and Anne was sure she caught a glimpse of a rather self-satisfied look being shared by

Mr. Everton Cormick and Lady Gertrude. She frowned momentarily, wondering what the two of them were up to. Were they perhaps trying to throw her and Henry together in some way?

As a companion to Miss Spencer, she was not in London to further her own marriage prospects – and even if she had been, she would not set her cap at a man younger than herself even if Henry was only younger than her by a year or two. His shyness made him seem much younger than his years, and though it was pleasant enough to talk literature with him that did not seem to her to be a strong enough foundation for a match. She also knew that Henry Cormick had a penchant for gambling, and she had no desire to wed a man who might spend every penny at the tables.

She excused herself from the little group, with the excuse of putting Henry's book away in her room. She was glad of the momentary escape from the now crowded room. It seemed that everyone in London had an agenda – whether for themselves, or for someone else – and she wished that Lady Gertrude and Mr. Cormick had not settled upon her for whatever schemes they had in mind. All she wished was to be able to see her current charge wed, and to then return to her family. She had seen enough of Society now to know she did not seek it and would prefer a quiet life back in Devon.

Anne made her way back downstairs. She paused in the doorway, watching everyone for a moment or two. She wished she could enjoy the easy friendship that Mr. Cormick and Lady Gertrude seemed to share. They were as comfortable talking and laughing together as any two old friends could be. They made a fine match, his tall fairness complimenting her tiny frame and dark coloring. They were like night and day, but they fit together perfectly. She would not be surprised if by the end of the Season that the two were affianced – whatever protestations to the contrary that Lady Gertrude might make. Anne couldn't help feeling a little jealous of the connection between them.

Miss Spencer was holding court by the window, with a number of silly young men hanging on her every word, though she only had eyes for Lord Wilson, who still stood at the fireplace, but was now talking with Lord Crowley. Mrs. Spencer was talking quietly with the Duchess of Dorley and her daughter, Lady Isabelle Painter. The duchess and Mrs. Spencer were so engrossed in their conversation, that they had failed to notice that Lady Isabelle was staring at Lord Crowley, as if he were the answer to all her girlish dreams.

Anne couldn't help thinking that despite the gentility of the event that it was all rather tawdry. She glanced at the clock, wondering how much longer she would have to bear it. It chimed for the quarter hour, and Anne sighed, knowing that there was still a further three quarters of an hour before anyone would even consider taking their leave.

CHAPTER FOUR

Everton was pleased with Henry. He had acquitted himself well at the Spencers' At Home. Lending Miss Knorr that book had been a very deft touch on his brother's part, something Everton had not thought of. Perhaps Henry really did like her? That he had thought of her in such a way was very encouraging indeed. However, Everton was beginning to wish he didn't have to be so present at every event. He enjoyed a party, as much as the next man, but being forced to attend them to look out for another was not as enjoyable as going for oneself.

Lady Gertrude was sweet and kind, and she was all too perceptive for a girl of her age. He enjoyed her company and the witty things she said. She was a fine dancer and had a sensible head on her shoulders. She knew she was there to find a husband, but she seemed determined not to rush into anything. He thought that very wise of her. Too many marriages were made rapidly in the first flush of infatuation and young girls often came to regret the choices they had made.

Lady Gertrude was of course luckier than most young women, as her family would not pressure her into marriage with someone just to further their own aims. The Duchy of Compton was wealthy enough, and they needed no additional noble blood to enrich their own. He was sure that the duke and duchess would let her wed someone she wished – as they had done with her brother. However, Everton worried that there might not be any young man that would live up to the requirements the feisty young woman held for her future husband. She was certainly not likely to accept anything less than she thought she deserved.

He had made Wycliffe a promise, to look out for Lady Gertrude and he would keep it - but he did not wish to enjoy the London of debutantes. All those silly girls, like Miss Spencer, all vying to beat one another to win the prize of the perfect husband. It was all so old-fashioned and dull. That he also had to watch out for Henry was another burden he'd rather not have to bear. His younger brother had already burnt through his quarterly allowance and had sent begging letters to their father for more. He would be glad when Wycliffe returned and Henry retired to the country for some peace and quiet, so Everton could return to his own life once more.

As he tied his cravat, ready to attend another evening's entertainment, Everton's gaze dropped to the miniature he kept by his bed of Katherine. Her sweet face was as lovely to him now as it had ever been. He picked it up and traced a finger over the soft lines of her cheek and tried not to remember how pale and gaunt she had looked in her final days as she battled so hard against the influenza that had taken her from him and from her family.

It was beyond cruel that Miss Spencer was the very image of her – yet had none of Katherine's kindness and grace. Every time he saw the rather vain and unpleasant girl, he felt a pang of guilt and pain. He forgot for a moment that she was not his Katherine, and then she would speak, or give someone a disdainful look and he would remember that his love was gone, and that Miss Spencer only resembled her on the outside. And because of his promise to Wycliffe, he was forced to see her over and over and over again.

Then there was his brother. Everton had no clue what to do about Henry. His mother and father were determined that a bride would settle down his more wayward tendencies. Everton was not so sure. Henry was not one for parties and balls. His favored activities were generally quiet, solitary even. But his gambling was a problem. The lad seemed to have no idea when to stop, or when his losses were too great, and Everton feared for him.

It was a delight to see him with Miss Knorr, who was one of the sweetest women alive. She was patient and even-tempered. She liked literature and poetry and seemed to share similar tastes to Henry in that regard. Yet something nagged at Everton, that the match wasn't quite right. He remembered holding Miss Knorr in his arms, waltzing with her at Wycliffe's wedding, and again at Almack's and wondered if a woman like her would truly be happy with a boy like his brother? She was quiet, true enough, and he got the impression that she was unimpressed by the Season and its purpose to find suitable husbands for the young women of *the Ton*. Yet she, contrarily perhaps, seemed to enjoy good company, music and dancing – things Henry disdained.

But it was not his place to decide. It seemed that the pair had struck up some manner of friendship at least, and Henry was less unwilling than he had been to attend at least some of the events this year. Tonight, they were to attend a new play. He doubted if anyone going actually cared about whether it was good or bad. Sitting in the most prominent position one could afford was the purpose of attending the theatre during the Season. Whispers passed between the boxes and along the rows of seats, condemning or praising the women's choice of gowns and remarking upon the gentlemen's choice of who to escort.

"Are you ready?" Henry asked, poking his head around the door. "I don't want to be late. I wish to discuss the script with Miss Knorr before the performance."

Everton smiled. His brother had never hurried him to anything before in his life. Perhaps there was hope that there was a match there after all. He grabbed his coat, and the two men went down the stairs, crossed the hall and went out onto the street. The carriage awaited them, and they got inside. "You like her, don't you?" Everton asked as it pulled into traffic. "Miss Knorr, I mean."

"I enjoy discussing things with her," Henry said.

"She is very intelligent and comes up with some excellent points."

"Is that all?" Everton asked. "Do you not also notice that she is pretty, with a lovely smile and roses in her cheeks?"

"Oh, I'm sure she is comely enough," Henry said, "but I am not concerned with that. What use is a pretty face if there is no intelligence or perception beneath it?"

Everton shook his head in disbelief. His brother was such an unusual creature. Everton doubted that Henry would notice if Aphrodite herself was stood in front of him, begging him for his love. What chance did any mere mortal possess?

They reached the theatre and entered the foyer, where Lady Gertrude and Miss Jessup were awaiting them. "Oh, I am so glad you are here early," she said tucking an arm through his. "I do so love to be here before the auditorium fills. There is such a sense of anticipation when in an empty theatre."

"My brother wishes to discuss the script with Miss Knorr. Have she and Miss Spencer arrived yet?"

"No, I doubt they'll be here early," Lady Gertrude said. "Poor Henry, I fear you may be very disappointed. Miss Spencer likes to make an entrance once all eyes are upon her."

Henry frowned and disappeared. Everton escorted Lady Gertrude and Miss Jessup inside. He had never been into a theatre when it was virtually empty before and was surprised to find that Lady Gertrude was quite right. There was a peculiar sense of excitement at being the first in the vast space, looking out over all the empty chairs and the curtained stage. The trio watched as people began to file in. Lady Gertrude noted a number of faces she knew and waved. A few friends came to talk with them in their box, and eventually, just before the play was about to start, Miss Spencer arrived with Miss Knorr walking demurely a few steps behind.

Everyone glanced up at the box at their arrival, as Miss Spencer had obviously planned. She smiled and waved at a few people and then made a performance of taking her seat. Everton shared a grin with Miss Knorr behind the young woman's back. "Good evening," he whispered to her.

"And to you," she replied. "Where is Henry?"

"He was disappointed you weren't here when we arrived. I think he went to find some friends. I am sure he'll be here shortly."

But Henry did not appear in the box during the first act, nor the second. In fact, it was clear within moments of the play beginning that his brother had left the theatre altogether. Everton had never been more disappointed in his brother, and for his brother. Henry had been so keen to attend tonight, had been sure that he would find an intellectual pursuit to his liking with someone whose company he enjoyed. Yet, there had been no time for that. And because he could not enjoy the night the way he wished to Henry had simply abandoned it.

The play was not good. Everyone agreed that as they filed out of the theatre. Perhaps Henry had been the wisest of them all to disappear before it had even begun.

Miss Spencer was, as usual, surrounded by a group of admirers. Miss Knorr stood alone, to one side, waiting for her. Everton shrugged on his coat and joined her by the carriage. "I am sorry about Henry," he said softly. "He came with me and seemed very keen on seeing you. It must have been something very important that called him away."

"You need not make excuses for him," Miss Knorr said with a wry smile.

"You two seem to have grown close," Everton said with a shrug. "I've not seen him enjoy anyone's company so much."

"And you need not flatter me with false praise." She laughed. "Mr. Cormick, your brother and I are barely even friends. We share some similar tastes in our reading, but nothing more. I doubt your brother is aware if I am a woman or a man, to tell you the truth. He is not the sort of person that cares of such things."

It was a peculiar thing to say, but as Everton let her words wander around his mind, he realized she was right. Henry did not care if someone was man or woman. His only concern was could he discuss the matters he thought important with them. He was the sort of man that would have been happy cloistered away in a university, with only books and other fusty academics to discuss the world and all its ills with. He wondered if it might be time to remind his parents of that fact – Henry did not belong here, amongst *the Ton* and he would not make a good husband to anyone.

"You are a very wise young lady," he said to Miss Knorr, who flushed at his sincere compliment.

"I don't know about that, but I have spent enough time watching people and how they act to see past the façade – at least some of the time."

"Are people all so deceptive?"

"Not all. Some are as easy to read as an open book – but others, they hide everything behind a mask," Miss Knorr said, glancing around at her charge. "Take Miss Spencer, she knows she has little but her beauty and her fortune to commend her. She knows she must seem to be more than that, and so she plays her part – that of a silly, sweet debutante."

"And those who court her?"

"Ah, now they are simply fools," Miss Knorr said with a smile. "They see only what they wish to see – and they spend their days coming up with bigger and more impressive boasts in order to try and win a woman that does not exist."

"And Lady Gertrude, and myself?" Everton asked, not sure if he wished to hear her thoughts or not.

"Well, Lady Gertrude is true to herself. She has learned much in the past year. Where she might have put on a mask in the past to get her way, she now knows that she will be more likely to get what she really wants if she is herself. She has grown wise like an owl." She paused, looking up at him shyly, then ducked her head away as if she did not wish to speak of him.

"And me," Everton prompted her. "What do you see when you look at me?"

"You are a mystery," Miss Knorr said. "Your mask is very good. You seem to be gregarious, generous and at the very heart of everything. Yet I am never sure if you are really with us or not. At least a part of you is often else-where, especially when you look at Miss Spencer. If I did not know you are not a fool, I would be tempted to think that you are as besotted as every other man in London."

CHAPTER FIVE

M*ay 1820, London*

THAT SHE HAD BEEN SO FRANK with Mr. Cormick
concerned Anne in the days that followed. She was not
normally one to share her innermost thoughts. She did
not know what to think of Henry's early departure, in
truth. In recent weeks he had seemed solicitous and
considerate, yet he was always a hundred miles away,
thinking on something new and that he wanted to keep
entirely to himself. But his behavior obviously concerned
his brother. Mr. Cormick was, like her, condemned to
forever make apologies for his charge.

It was no surprise to Anne that Miss Spencer had
already managed to upset so many of the young women
and their mothers here in London this Season. Miss
Spencer did not seem to understand the need for allies
amongst her own sex. If it were not for Lady Gertrude's

continuing acquaintanceship, the invitations would have begun to slow and the opportunities for Miss Spencer to find a husband would be narrowing. Yet, Miss Spencer showed no gratitude for the largesse that she was being offered.

There were still young men infatuated with her, but even they seemed to disappear once they had spent more than a few suppers in Miss Spencer's company. She simply did not know how to be gracious, to be interested in others – or anything much other than her own desperate search for the right husband.

Thankfully, Lord Wilson was one of those who seemed immune to Miss Spencer's less attractive traits or was perhaps not bright enough to notice them. He seemed to worship her, and Anne found herself wishing every day for a swift engagement and nuptials so she would be free. She was therefore delighted when she heard that Lord Wilson had requested an audience with Miss Spencer's father. Mr. Spencer would be travelling from Northumberland imminently so it could take place.

Anne prayed every night that an arrangement would be made, knowing that to do so was selfish and wrong on her part. She had never before prayed for something for her own gain, and she hoped that the fact that her wish would make both Miss Spencer and, for a time at least, Lord Wilson happy made her sin less grave. Miss Spencer grew more testy as the days passed and her father had not yet arrived "When will he be here?" she demanded of her mother. "Does he not care one jot for me?"

"He will be here as soon as the horses can carry him

here," her mother assured her. "He is not doing it on purpose. You know as well as anyone that the weather in the North at this time of year can be most inclement. In the meantime, you must get ready for the ball tonight."

Miss Spencer sighed heavily and flounced up to her bedchamber. Anne followed on reluctantly. The young woman was seated at her dressing table, unpinning her hair when Anne arrived. Anne picked up her ivory-handled brush and began to ease it through the lengths of golden hair. "Ow," Miss Spencer cried when Anne came across a particularly difficult knot.

"Hold still, it will be done in a moment," Anne said as she took the length of hair and held it firmly a little way away from the girl's scalp and pulled the brush through the ends over and over until the knot was gone.

Miss Spencer stared at herself in the mirror, pulling at eyelids and pinching at her cheeks to make them color. She pursed her lips and tossed her glorious mane of hair. "Do you think he will grow tired of me?" she asked Anne, looking unexpectedly unsure of herself.

Anne gave her a reassuring smile. "He is besotted with you."

"But is that enough?" she asked. "Will that remain enough? We both know I am not a kind woman, that I have little feeling for the feelings of others."

Anne was surprised at Miss Spencer's sudden self-awareness. She had shown little desire to look within in the time Anne had been her companion. "That is something you can perhaps change," she suggested gently. "Why go through life alone, when you could have loving friends and an adoring husband?"

"It is easy for you," Miss Spencer said, turning to look at Anne. "You are pretty and sweet and good. It is who you are. I have to work so hard to be any of those things."

"Yet you are the one who has a fine young man who wishes to marry you," Anne reminded her. "For all my sweet goodness I am unlikely to ever find a husband. I am too old – at just twenty-four years of age, I am an old maid."

"How do you do it? How do you stay so calm when others are so foolish?" Miss Spencer asked. "I wish to be wed, but secretly I fear that a lifetime with Lord Wilson may be even harder to bear than one with my parents. At least they let me be – most of the time."

"What would you rather?" Anne asked as she turned to put the curling tongs in the fire.

"Someone with their own interests, who doesn't need me to compliment and praise them all the time. I would like them to not exactly be cold, but to perhaps be more like me and know that love isn't always the answer to every problem. I do not wish for a monster, but I do not long for romance and flowers. It seems so false to me."

Anne smiled, as Henry Cormick's face sprang into her mind unbidden. She couldn't help thinking that the person Miss Spencer had just described was the very image of him. It wasn't that he didn't care; he just didn't see the point in pretending something he did not think or feel. "Do you like books, Miss Spencer?" she asked as she took the tongs from the fire and began to curl Miss Spencer's hair into tight ringlets around her face.

"I do. What makes you ask?"

"It is just that I was recently lent a rather interesting

one. I shall pass it on to you, and then perhaps once you've read it you could pass it back to my friend." She hurried to her room and returned with the book, handing it to Miss Spencer.

"I've read it. It is a wonderful book," she said taking it and flicking through the pages. "Your friend annotated this? The one you are so often talking with? With the dark curls and brooding look about him." Such a description of Henry made Anne smile. He rather reminded her of a spaniel puppy, so to hear Miss Spencer say he was brooding seemed overly fanciful.

"Henry Cormick, yes he did," Anne said holding back a giggle. "He has some very interesting ideas about literature. I think you might find him good to talk to. He certainly does not feign interest where he has none."

"I should like that," Miss Spencer said. "I have seen the two of you talking from time to time. You look to have very passionate discussions."

"Oh, we do. Henry is not shy in his opinions and encourages me to be bolder with my own," Anne admitted.

"I should like that. I hate having to pretend to be silly and not have thoughts of my own in order to placate men with nothing in their heads but their own importance. Why are men permitted to be whoever they actually are, yet women are forced into a mold – whether they fit within it or not?"

Anne did not have an answer to such a question. Miss Spencer was quite right, of course. Women were expected to conform to Society's ideas of what made a perfect wife. It stood to reason that not all girls were able to do this – as all men were not able to be the same. Yet men were permitted their differences. A man could grow old without ever marrying if he desired without being condemned. A man could follow whatever path he wished, at least to some extent – though there were many forced into positions they'd rather not be in due to family concerns. Yet if they were cantankerous, that was permitted. If they were easily angered, nobody stopped them from airing their temper. But a woman should be sweet and polite at all times, no matter how bored or unfulfilling her life as a wife and mother might be to her.

She finished pinning Miss Spencer's hair, feeling that she had been permitted to see into the young woman's soul for the very first time. It was not an entirely easy image to process, but Anne now understood her young charge better. It was not that Miss Spencer was spoiled and unkind, but that she struggled to be what was expected of young women in Society. Anne could understand that. As someone who was a little shy and very bookish, she struggled from time to time herself. Miss Spencer's concerns were harder to get past than a mere preference for a quiet life, though.

After she'd helped Miss Spencer into her gown, Anne hurried to her own rooms to dress for the ball. She washed her face and re-pinned her own hair. Her hair thankfully held its curl well enough to not need to be tonged anew. She chose a green velvet gown from her armoire. The color suited her dark coloring well and did much to offset the ruddiness of her cheeks. While other young women had to pinch themselves over and over or use rouge to add color to their peaches and cream complexions, Anne was a true English rose with her rosy cheeks and red lips.

"Miss Knorr," Miss Spencer said as they got into the carriage, their long, hooded evening capes flowing behind them, "may I call you Anne? I hear all of the young women of our acquaintance calling their companions by their names, and vice versa. Why do we not do that?"

"I do not know," Anne said, "but I would be happy to call you Caroline and have you call me Anne." The girl smiled at her nervously. Anne took her hand and squeezed it. "It will be quite alright," she assured her. "Whatever happens, it will be for the best."

Caroline nodded. They drove to the ball in silence, but Caroline clung to Anne's hand tightly. Anne marveled at how she had so misread the young woman in her care. Caroline was not selfish or vain – though she had been spoiled. She was forthright, blunt, clever - and knew that those were traits not much admired in young women. It must have been so hard for her to pretend to be otherwise – no wonder she was always so angry and frustrated.

The ball was already underway when they arrived. Caroline was soon mobbed by eager young men, as the young women of *the Ton* frowned at her. Anne spied Lady Gertrude, Mr. Cormick and the rumpled figure of Henry on the other side of the dance floor. She took Caroline aside. "Keep one dance, before supper free," she told her, then made her way through the crowds to her friends who greeted her warmly.

"Henry, would you do me a favor," she asked him once the pleasantries were complete. "Miss Spencer has nobody to take her into supper tonight. Would you perhaps do her the honor?"

Henry gave her a perplexed look but nodded. "If you wish me to," he said amiably enough. Anne thought that she saw Mr. Cormick and Lady Gertrude frown, but when she looked back at them, both were smiling as widely as ever.

"Come and meet her, I don't think the two of you have ever really been properly introduced," Anne said, shepherding Henry away from them and towards Caroline.

"Did you like Vampyre?" he asked her as they made their way through the crowds and drew closer to where Miss Spencer stood.

"I did, but not as much as I enjoyed the Modern Prometheus," Anne said, seeing Caroline smile as she overheard the topic of their conversation. "I think there were aspects of human nature that Mary Shelley captured that Polidori did not."

"I disagree," Henry said bristling a little as he often did when others disagreed with him.

"I do, too," Caroline said. "I think Polidori is by far the better observer of mankind."

And with that, the two were lost. Anne smiled, glad she had been right. Caroline simply needed someone who would value her forthright opinions and would not care if she were a man or a woman, simply that she cared enough to think.

"Whatever have you done?" Lady Gertrude asked as Anne rejoined their small party. "I've never seen Henry look like that. He's happy and angry all at once."

"And Miss Spencer actually looks as though she cares what he says," Miss Jessup marveled. "She looks positively radiant."

Anne grinned. "I learned something about Caroline earlier today – and it reminded me that Henry and she have much in common." She paused then smiled. "She thinks he has a brooding look about him."

Lady Gertrude shook her head. "Well, there's no accounting for what others think, is there," she marveled.

CHAPTER SIX

E verton didn't know whether to laugh or stare open-mouthed at the way his brother seemed to have come alive. The only other time Henry had seemed to be so delighted, so engrossed in anything was when he had been at university, arguing with his tutors and peers alike about some pedantic point only he cared about. And here he was, at a ball, in a heated but obviously much enjoyed discussion – by both parties involved. Everton had thought he'd enjoyed conversing with Miss Knorr, but it was clear just how much more he was enjoying his heated discussion with Miss Spencer.

"How did you know that would happen?" he asked Miss Knorr.

"I did not know for certain," she admitted. "But I must confess I hoped. Caroline was so honest with me earlier and as she spoke, I closed my eyes and thought of what she was saying – rather than who was saying it."

"And it reminded you of Henry."

"It did," she said. "They are very alike. If Caroline

were a man, she would probably have been a scholar – as Henry longs to be."

"He does?" Everton asked. Henry had never said such a thing – but then Henry never said much about anything – he assumed nobody wished to hear his thoughts on any matter, having been told to be quiet so many times throughout his young life. He was simply too passionate about his singular interests, and it was off-putting for those around him to hear one of his monologues.

"Yes, I think so. He speaks very fondly of his time at university – how he felt able to be himself there."

"I have suspected as much, but why has he never spoken of it to us?"

"That I cannot say," Miss Knorr said politely. "Perhaps you might have an idea why he would feel it difficult to say such a thing?"

Everton fell silent. It was clear enough to him why Henry would not have said such a thing. Throughout their lives, both boys had been groomed to enter their father's enterprises. They had been sent to the finest schools in the country. Both had attended Oxford and then had followed dutifully in their father's footsteps ever since. The work suited Everton. He enjoyed the cut and thrust of commerce, and the challenge of finding new markets and increasing the family's wealth. But such things bored Henry. He had been unhappy for years.

"Perhaps I should speak with my father on Henry's behalf," he said. "Though what he will say, I simply cannot imagine."

Miss Knorr gave him a sad smile. "It should be Henry

that says something, not you. He needs to learn to speak up for what he wants."

"But he will not, you know him as well as I do – if not perhaps better," Everton admitted. "He will never gainsay my father."

"Mayhaps if he knows he has your support, he might find the courage to do so," Miss Knorr said with a little shrug.

Everton pondered what she had said, as he danced with Lady Gertrude, then Miss Jessup and finally with Miss Knorr once more. He had purposefully claimed the dance before supper on her card so they might speak some more – and so that she would have someone to escort her into the dining room. With Henry otherwise engaged, he felt it his duty to ensure Miss Knorr was not in any way left out. Yet though he felt bad for her, Everton couldn't help but smile to see his brother so content.

Despite Lord Wilson's obvious unhappiness at being usurped, Henry and Miss Spencer were still discussing something animatedly, with many hand gestures, contorted expressions and occasional explosive outbursts. It was as if neither of them had even noticed the man. It must have been hard for Bertie to understand. One day he was the only man Miss Spencer seemed to care for, and suddenly it was as if he had never existed to her. It was not a particularly ladylike trait, but it was one he had seen in his brother on many occasions. Once caught up in a new passion, he would be lost to anything that had gone before it. It seemed that Miss Spencer was the same.

"Poor Bertie," Lady Gertrude said as they went into

the supper room, glancing over at the red-faced earl. "He does not know what he did wrong."

"Do you think she will return her affections to him?" Miss Jessup asked.

"I do not think she really had any," Miss Knorr said knowingly. "But it is quite clear that he did. I feel sad for him."

"Do you not mind for yourself?" Everton asked Miss Knorr as they sat down.

"Why should I mind?" she asked him, genuinely surprised by the question.

"I had thought that you and my brother had a mutual understanding."

She laughed. "We do, I suppose – as much as dear Henry could. I was interesting enough not to bore him," she said sagely. "But I don't think I could ever have managed more than that."

"I am sorry," Everton said.

"That your matchmaking, with Lady Gertrude came to nought?" she asked with a twinkle in her eye.

Everton felt color flood his cheeks. "You knew?"

"It was hard not to see how much you tried to throw us together," Miss Knorr said, clearly amused by his discomfiture.

They sat in companionable silence for a few moments. Everton shook his head from time to time, as a smile played over his lips. "I am sorry," he said eventually.

"Do not be," Miss Knorr said. "I am flattered that you would wish me to be a part of your family." She paused. "But I am interested in why you seem so determined to marry off your much younger brother – when you hide behind Lady Gertrude in order to avoid even the merest hint of speculation about whether you will or will not choose a bride yourself."

Everton's mouth dropped wide open. He had not expected that. "That was very direct," he said.

"Perhaps I am taking a lesson from my charge, mayhaps from Henry. But do you not think there is a little too much subterfuge in Society? Things might get managed much more quickly and more to everyone's satisfaction if we could all be a little more honest?"

She wasn't wrong. But Everton wasn't sure if he was ready to answer her question. He tried to think of ways to explain that wouldn't seem rude or utterly maudlin and failed. He looked at her sweet face and found himself impressed by the strong woman beneath. "You need not tell me," she said. "It is, after all, none of my business. I am perhaps too curious for my own good."

He took a deep breath. "I was affianced, some years ago now. My Katherine died of influenza, mere weeks before we were supposed to be wed."

"Ah," Miss Knorr said, reaching out and placing her dainty hand over his giant paw tenderly. "I am sorry. I should not have asked."

"No, I don't mind," he said, looking into her kindly eyes, and was surprised to find that he was telling the truth. He truly did not mind her asking. "Perhaps I have been too silent for too long."

With that supper was over and everyone made their way back into the ballroom. The orchestra began to play, and people scurried around trying to find partners. Everton retreated to the back room, where a card game was in progress. It made a change not to find his brother at the tables, but he sat down and took a hand. He wondered what it was about Miss Knorr that made people open up to her. She had gotten to the very crux of who both Henry and Miss Spencer were, seeing their similarities and their compatibility. And she had made him admit that Katherine was dead.

Saying it out loud to Miss Knorr had somehow made it real. It was almost as if the past three years of never speaking of it, of Katherine, had been a way of pretending that it wasn't true. That one day his Katherine would reappear, and everything would be as it was. Tonight, that feeling was not there any longer. He felt a peculiar mixture of relief and grief.

He threw his hand down on the table, stood up and made his excuses to leave. He bade goodnight to Lady Gertrude, waved at his brother who did not even notice him as he was so wrapped up in his continuing discussion with Miss Spencer. He nodded politely to Miss Knorr who was dancing with a red-coated army captain.

He walked out into the street and wandered without any thought to his direction. He walked along streets and avenues, through the elegant garden squares and out onto the busy thoroughfares. He tried not to think, but images of Katherine crowded his mind. Her face the day he'd proposed, so full of hope and happiness. The way she'd looked the first time he ever saw her, at Almack's in her finest ball gown, dancing, her head thrown back and a broad smile upon her face. And the way she had looked as she took her last breath, as he held her hand tightly and willed her to stay with him.

He had loved her with all his heart. But as he walked through the dark streets of London, he realized that he was not that man any longer. The man that had loved Katherine had been full of life. He had wanted to experience every pleasure, every joy – even every sadness, except the one that had taken her from him. The man he was now denied himself happiness. He felt himself to be undeserving – and that it would be a betrayal of her memory if he found the kind of joy that he'd known with her, with anyone else.

And so, he had learned to keep everyone at a distance. He had vowed to never love again.

But who was that punishing? Was it punishing the influenza that had taken Katherine from him? Was it punishing a cruel God who had seen fit to reclaim one of his angels early? Could he have done anything differently? Was it really his fault that she had been lost to him and everyone else who loved her?

The simple answer was the only person being punished by his refusal to let her go, was himself. Katherine would never have wished for such a life for him. She had loved him utterly. She would be ashamed of the man he was now if she could see him.

He stopped in the middle of the road and stared up to the heavens. "What should I do?" he asked her, knowing he would get no reply – but wishing on every star in the heavens that she could tell him what to do, how to live without her. He'd been surviving, but he could not go on this way forever.

He slowly retraced his steps, back to Almack's. The revelers were making their way out of the doors and into their carriages. Lady Gertrude and Miss Jessup were amongst the last to leave. He smiled ruefully at them as he stepped forward to open their carriage door. Lady Gertrude placed a gloved hand over his. "Are you alright?" she asked him gently.

"I think I will be," he said. "Though it might take me a while."

She gave him a sad smile and leaned over and kissed him on the cheek. "Be careful, you'll ruin your reputation," he teased.

"Everyone in *the Ton* knows you are as good as a brother to me. I doubt anyone will think anything of it," she said getting into the carriage, followed by Miss Jessup. He shut the door behind them. Lady Gertrude leaned out of the window. "Darling Everton, I know you loved Katherine – but is it not time to let her rest?"

"I think you might be right," he said. "It will not be easy though."

"No, especially with a living, breathing reminder here every day to drive you half mad."

"You noticed the resemblance between Miss Spencer and Katherine, too, then."

"I did. But other than their looks, they are nothing alike. You know that don't you?"

He nodded. "I do. Katherine was fond of Henry, but he drove her to distraction at times. She would never have gotten lost in discussion with him the way Miss Spencer did tonight."

"It was rather remarkable, wasn't it?" Lady Gertrude said shaking her lovely head. "She has not missed the opportunity to dance even once this Season – yet tonight, she rebuffed every gentleman on her card in favor of Henry. They will be quite the talk of *the Ton* tomorrow – a veritable scandal."

"I know, and I cannot say how glad I am of it. Perhaps Henry has finally found someone he can be himself with."

"And Miss Spencer. She was quite a different person tonight. I might have to completely change my opinion of her," Lady Gertrude said with a grin.

CHAPTER SEVEN

"How could you be so careless?" a red-faced Mrs. Spencer railed at her daughter over lunch. Anne was surprised at how angry the usually kindly older woman was, though Caroline seemed to barely notice; she continued to eat her soup as if her mother was not even speaking to her – much less yelling loud enough that the entire street might hear. "To spend the entire evening with just one gentleman? And to ignore the one man we know has intentions towards you?" Mrs. Spencer's eyes flashed with fire. The fact that her daughter seemed unperturbed only served to make her more angry.

She turned her gaze upon Anne, who had been trying to keep her head down, and stay out of the matter, though she knew that as the girl's companion she was as much to blame as Caroline herself – if not more so. Her position existed solely to protect her charge from such gossip and the behaviors that might lead to it. "And what sort of a companion are you?" Mrs. Spencer demanded of her. "That you would let a young woman do such a thing. I did not take you on so my daughter could be the subject of malicious gossip throughout the town. I should send you packing without a character."

"There was nothing untoward," Anne tried to protest, though she knew there was no defense. She should have insisted Caroline at least dance with a few other men present at Almack's the night before for propriety's sake – but it had been so nice to see Caroline and Henry together. They truly were two of a kind, a matched pair. "They were in a room full of people. They did nothing but talk to one another." It was true, but Anne knew it was insufficient defense. There were rules to be lived by, and Society did not approve when its rules were broken.

"I know," Mrs. Spencer exploded, as if the explanation made it so much worse. Anne had to admit, that the outcry had occurred much more swiftly and was much worse than she could have ever expected. There had been a number of so-called friends who had seen fit to arrive at the house this morning, and others who had written faux-sympathetic letters, all purporting to be concerned for Caroline's reputation. Each one had gleefully regaled the scandal of Caroline choosing to spend her entire evening in conversation with Henry Cormick, and Lord Wilson's embarrassment at being so slighted.

"All ruddy night – ignoring everyone else," Mrs. Spencer added, then paused for a moment and looked back at her daughter. "Lord Wilson will not stand for such an insult. You can kiss goodbye to any hopes you might have had for a match with him. Your father will be furious to find he has come all this way for nothing."

"We do not know that he no longer wishes to be affianced to me," Caroline said looking up from her soup briefly. Of course, she was right. They had not heard a word from the man who was supposedly so affronted by her behavior – but Anne knew that was probably not a good indication as to whether or not he was upset or not, even if Caroline seemed unconcerned about that. A gentleman would not show his feelings in public. He would be licking his wounds in private.

"Because you did not speak to him," Mrs. Spencer spat. "But let me tell you, my girl, he'll not stand for such treatment. No man could. You've cuckolded him before you're even wed."

"Do not be so dramatic, Mama," Caroline said calmly. "I shall speak with him tonight at Lady Hannover's card party. I shall smooth everything out. You shall see."

Anne knew that Caroline could be cold, but she truly did not seem to understand why Lord Wilson might not be open to even speaking with her at tonight's event. Anne would be surprised if he even attended. Even if his heart was not affected by Caroline's treatment of him, his pride would most certainly have been badly damaged by her snubbing of him the previous evening, and Lord Wilson did care very deeply for Caroline, even if she did not feel the same way. "Caroline, he may not even attend," Anne said softly. "I do not know if there is a way to smooth things over. I am sorry, your mother is right, I should not have let you remain with Mr. Cormick all evening. I have let you down terribly."

"Nonsense, if you had not lent me his book, I would

not have enjoyed my evening at all," Caroline said simply and without any hint of emotion at all. "I do so hate having to dance and pretend to be gay and opinion-less all the time."

"You can be as opinionated as you like, once you are wed," Mrs. Spencer said, almost apoplectic now. "Until then, you need to abide by the rules. No man will marry you after last night's performance. I can assure you of that."

"Mama, you are wrong," Caroline said simply. "Lord Wilson will. Perhaps even Mr. Cormick will. Then there are any number of other silly men and old men who would be delighted to have a pretty bride. I shall simper and be what is expected of me again, I promise."

Somewhat placated, Mrs. Spencer rose from the table having not touched her lunch. She swept from the room with the hauteur of a duchess. It was sometimes hard to remember that she came from much more humble stock. Caroline grinned at Anne, who was shaking her head – wondering how someone as clever as Caroline could have gotten everything so utterly wrong. Society might appear to welcome her, but she had always been on thin ice due to her background. She had upset many people – and they would not easily forgive her, no matter how well she behaved going forward.

"At least she did not put you out on the streets," Caroline said in a rather tasteless joke.

Anne sighed heavily. "No, she did not. Though she should have done. I am at fault. I should have interrupted you – at least from time to time."

"I am glad you did not. I cannot think of a time when

I have been happier," Caroline admitted. "Mr. Cormick can be most insightful – and also infuriating. It was such a delight to have someone actually listen to my thoughts and take them seriously."

"I understand that," Anne said. "Truly, I do. But Society frowns upon such things – and I should have done more to ensure that your name was not linked to any scandal. I feel that my intervention is to blame. They will not be so quick to forgive and forget as you hope, I fear."

"Society means little to me, Anne. I do not see the point in all of its rules and prescriptions. Much as I dislike my Mama's insistence that I be a polite and demure young lady, it is not who I am. Why do I have to pretend to be something I am not, in order to marry a man who will not like me once we are wed – because he knows nothing of the real person underneath the lies?"

She was right of course. Everything about the Season was designed to ensnare and entrap. It was only afterwards that anyone really found out what bargain they had struck. If Caroline could make a match with someone who accepted her for precisely who she was, would she not be happier? Would her husband not be more content? "Do you truly think that possible?" Anne asked.

"I did not before last night," Caroline admitted and almost looked a little dreamy as she recalled the events of the night before. It was quite clear that Henry Cormick had not just touched her mind, but her heart – such as it was – as well. If Anne hadn't been so concerned for the young woman and her future, she would have been delighted for her. It was not easy to find a true love match in Society. They were as rare as the finest rubies and emeralds.

"You truly like Henry Cormick?" Anne asked, astounded that this cold young woman might actually have found someone she could not only respect, but actually admire and hold genuine affection for.

"I do. He is not to everyone's taste, as I myself am not," she said with wry humor. "But he is clever and thoughtful, passionate and so very well-read. His opinions are carefully formed, and he argues them with force and vigor. He is the kind of man I could be myself with, I believe. He would encourage my intellect and would not mind if I disagreed with his conclusions – as long as I could explain sufficiently why."

Anne couldn't help herself, she chuckled. "Well, that is a turn of events I doubt anyone foresaw."

"You do not mind? I had thought that perhaps you were sweet on him yourself."

"No, I like Henry. He is, as you say, interesting and well-read. But he is not for me." An image of Everton Cormick flashed through Anne's mind. He too was interesting and well-read, and much more to Anne's taste – though she knew that he would never see anyone but his lost Katherine in that way again.

"Do you think I should write to Lord Wilson? Perhaps I can explain to him what happened, that I just got carried away with the intensity of my discussion with Mr. Cormick?" Caroline said, unexpectedly thoughtful. "I did not mean to snub him, or anyone else. Time simply got away from me."

"A letter might be a good idea, but I would not say that. A man in love does not wish to think that the object of his affections was caught up so totally by the conversation of another man."

"Oh," Caroline exclaimed, her frustration clear in the tone of her voice. "Why are men so ridiculously prideful? Why do they need lies to placate and soothe them? It makes no sense at all to me."

"I do not know, but they do seem to be most delicate about such matters," Anne said with a smile. "Oftentimes even more so than any jilted woman I have ever known."

"Will you help me to write something suitable? I do not wish him to think I do not like him. In my own way, I do. He is not as interesting as Mr. Cormick, nor as intelligent. But he is sweet enough. I must wed, and he is as good a choice as any."

"If Mr. Cormick does not show an interest in such a thing?" Anne probed.

Caroline did not respond, but the way her cheeks flushed told Anne that she would not be averse to such a match. Given the current circumstances, with the scandal the two had unwittingly caused, such a match might be the only option left open to her. Society did not like to have its rules broken – and the pressure on the young couple to conform and silence the scandal might just work in Caroline's favor. Even Henry Cormick, for all his non-conformity, would not be able to resist the full force of *the Ton*.

The pair made their way into the parlor and Anne sat down at the escritoire by the window. She took out paper and dipped a pen into the inkwell and started to write what she hoped would be an acceptable explanation for what had occurred the night before, that Caroline could send to Lord Wilson. It took the two of them six attempts to have something that told the truth, but also made it more palatable as Caroline was determined that she would not lie to Lord Wilson. They sealed it and had one of the kitchen lads deliver it to his house, and Anne prayed that he would be willing to accept it. They would find out if he could at the card party tonight.

The rest of the afternoon dragged interminably. Anne glanced at the clock on the mantel more often than she should have, as the pair played duets at the pianoforte, and painted watercolors to pass the time. Then there was the usual rush of preparations, newly pinned and curled hair, freshly pressed evening gowns to put on and then the carriage ride to Lady Hannover's Mayfair townhouse.

Anne had never been so nervous. A veritable swarm of insects seemed to have taken up residence in her belly, though Caroline seemed to be as unruffled as ever. When they walked into the salon, everyone fell silent. Anne had grown used to late entrances and all eyes being upon them, as Caroline had insisted upon it in order to make an impression – but it felt very different tonight.

Anne glanced around to see if Lord Wilson was in attendance but could not see his sturdy frame anywhere. She did see the smiling face of Lady Gertrude, who beckoned the two of them over to her table. "Miss Spencer, Miss Knorr," she said loudly, standing up and kissing Caroline's cheek and clasping Anne's hands affectionately. "I am so glad you could make it. The evening would not be the same without you." Such an endorsement from someone who was so highly regarded would not do Caroline any harm at all. Anne hoped that Lady Gertrude knew just how grateful she was for it.

People around them began to look away and resume their conversations, but there were still occasional side glances and whispers. Anne knew that Caroline was the subject of every tables' gossip. But then Lord Wilson arrived, and the silence as he crossed the room was deafening. Lady Gertrude smiled broadly, as if it was any other evening, as he made his way straight to them and bowed deeply. "Lady Gertrude, Miss Spencer, Miss Jessup, Miss Knorr," he said greeting them all in turn.

"Well, I am very happy to see you here," Lady Gertrude said. "Would you like to join us, to make up a four? Miss Jessup does not enjoy whist very much and Lady Hannover asked earlier if she might play the pianoforte for us all as we play." It was deftly done, and Anne couldn't help thinking that Lady Gertrude had been planning for just such an eventuality. She shot the young woman a grateful look. Lady Gertrude nodded and smiled in return.

"I should be delighted," Lord Wilson said, smiling happily as he took the seat that Miss Jessup vacated to make her way to the instrument at the other end of the room. Anne could see that everyone present that evening had been expecting him to either not attend, or to be so offended that he would ignore Miss Spencer. There were many in attendance that seemed quite put out that Lord Wilson seemed to bear Miss Spencer no ill will.

Lady Gertrude deftly cut the cards and then dealt

them each a hand. Lord Wilson took his cards, then leant closer to Caroline. "Thank you for your letter, Miss Spencer," he said quietly, his voice barely more than a whisper. "It was most kind of you."

"I wished you to know that it was nothing personal, of that I must assure you," Caroline said earnestly. "I can get so caught up sometimes, when discussing something I am interested in. I..." she tailed off, as if it was something she simply could not help – and Anne supposed that in many ways, she truly could not. She had been so lost in the moment that nothing else had existed for her.

"I think I am man enough to forgive you for that," he said generously. He truly was a very decent man, and Anne couldn't help feeling a little sorry for him. He would never be able to engage Caroline the way Henry Cormick did, but he truly did care for her. He wanted her to be happy.

"I am so glad," Caroline said, and Anne knew she meant it. In her own way, she did like Bertie Wilson. It was just a way that might not be enough for such a man, in the end.

CHAPTER EIGHT

As Kingsley, the family butler, appeared in the library with more letters regarding Henry's behavior the night before, Everton sighed heavily. He sliced them open with his ivory-handled letter knife and read the same words he'd been reading from friends and acquaintances all day. Everyone was aghast at the way Henry had monopolized Miss Spencer at Almack's. Young men who were put out that they had not been able to dance with Miss Spencer made it clear that they would not tolerate such behavior in the future. The grand dames of Society insisted he do something to protect the honor of our young women, though what Everton was supposed to do they left ambiguous in their outrage.

He shook his head. The whole thing seemed to have been blown out of proportion. What was really wrong with two unattached young people spending an evening talking together, in full view of all of Society? Why were the rules as they were? Why was it a scandal that a woman only dance with one man, or talk with him –

rather than if she danced with every man? And why were people who barely knew Bertie Wilson making threats to Henry's safety on his behalf? There was no arrangement, as far as Everton knew, between Miss Spencer and Lord Wilson. There were rumors that the two were to be affianced, but it had not yet occurred. There was no formal claim on the young woman's time, or her hand. If Bertie had been truly upset by Henry's monopolization of Miss Spencer, he should have interrupted them last night. He should have insisted upon Miss Spencer's company for the dances he had reserved on her card.

But Society etiquette ruled that would be a poor show – and so, he had done no such thing. He had simply looked on and looked sad. Bertie was not clever, but he was not a fool. He understood people. He had to have known that Miss Spencer's feelings for him were not the same as those he held for her. And he was the type to accept that if she did not care for him, that he was better off looking elsewhere. Oh, his pride would smart for a few days, but he would soon be falling in love with another young lady. It was the kind of man he was.

Yet, despite that, someone would have to be seen to be punished for the transgression – even though there was no real harm done. Everton would have to be seen to be acting upon the matter in place of his absent father, to discipline Henry and make him face up to the errors he had made. But what to do?

The bell rang for supper. Everton left the letters on the desk and made his way into the dining room. Henry appeared a few moments later, his hair disheveled as usual, his nose stuck in a book that he seemed reluctant to set down until the very moment the first course arrived. He marked his place by folding over a corner of the page, closed the book and set it on the table beside him. Everton frowned and took a deep breath. "We are going to have to do something," he said firmly.

"About what?" Henry said, distractedly as he took a spoonful of soup and slurped at it loudly.

"Your table manners for one," Everton retorted, annoyed that Henry was so unaware of the furor that had erupted since the ball last night. How could he be so oblivious? Did he truly not care about anything other than his own intellectual pursuits?

"I know to be more refined in public, you don't need to worry about them," Henry said with a grin.

"You are the most exasperating creature," Everton said shaking his head, his brother was incorrigible. "You do know that being out on the terrace with her alone couldn't have ruined her reputation more effectively, Henry?"

"Who? I've not been out on a terrace with anyone," Henry said distractedly as he continued to eat the rich oxtail broth that had been set before him.

"I know, I am talking about your conversation with Miss Spencer, last night," Everton explained patiently to his brother, doing all in his power to keep his annoyance from his voice. "You know that Society has rules. Why must you always seek to ignore them?"

"I do not mean to."

"I received word today, that the Lady Patronesses are to meet to discuss revoking our vouchers for the rest of the Season."

"I cannot say that disappoints me," Henry said with a mischievous grin. But when he glanced at Everton's angry expression, his face fell. "I did not mean to cause such a ruckus," he said with a nonchalant shrug. "We started talking, then all of a sudden the night was over. I truly do not see how having a conversation with someone, in full view of everyone, could possibly bring about their fall from grace."

"You truly do not, do you?" Everton said with a heavy sigh. "The man rumored to be about to ask Miss Spencer to marry him was in attendance at Almack's last night. He would have expected to dance with her; before supper, after supper and at the end of the night, so he might escort her home. Yet she did not dance with him, or anyone, all night. She talked. To you."

"So, she did not dance. I did not kiss her or hold her too tightly. I talked to her – about literature and science. Is that really so shocking to the grand dames of *the Ton?*"

"Given that I have received some twenty or more letters today, it would appear so." Everton knew there was no getting through to his brother about this. He would never understand – no matter how much Everton tried to explain. It made no sense to Henry, and so he was almost deaf to it. "You will have to apologize to Bertie, you know, at the very least. He would be within his rights to challenge you to a duel."

"But I'm terrible with a pistol, and even worse with a sword," Henry said naively. "Bertie knows that. He'd not do that, not to me."

"Don't you see, none of that matters, you dolt. It is

not a matter of whether he likes you or not, but that his honor – and Miss Spencer's honor – is at stake."

"But I don't want to fight Bertie. There's nothing to fight over."

"You might think that, but there is nobody else in London that does," Everton said exasperated. "You have to make amends – even if you think you did nothing wrong."

"And how, precisely do I do that?"

"You will have to ask for Miss Spencer's hand, before Bertie does. That way, her honor is protected and he may be able to save face."

"Fine, I shall do that, then," Henry said. He picked up his book, stood up, and opening the book to where he'd left off as he approached the table, he began to read as he walked out of the room.

Everton shook his head. Henry was a law unto himself. Yet, such lack of feeling about being forced to marry was concerning to Everton. He did not particularly like Miss Spencer, but she deserved better than his brother's nonchalance. And Henry had always been vehemently against the idea of being married. He often claimed that he saw little merit in it. Such indifference now seemed strange. True enough, Henry had come to London to please their parents and to pay lip-service to their demands that he find a wife, but nobody had expected him to actually find a bride.

Everton had held onto hope that Henry might change his mind, and that a match with Miss Knorr might interest his brother, as they seemed to have at least a few things in common – but it had been the slimmest of hopes. Henry was the very image of the English confirmed bachelor – eccentric and distracted. That he now seemed undaunted by the idea of marriage to Miss Spencer could only mean one thing. That Everton's little brother had finally found someone sufficiently like himself to actually want to spend time with them.

Grabbing the decanter of port and a glass from the table, Everton made his way into his father's study. He quickly penned a note to Lord Wilson, and a second to Miss Knorr, requesting an audience with Miss Spencer for Henry the next morning, sealed it, poured himself a glass of the rich red liquid and leant back in the high-backed leather chair and sipped it thoughtfully, wishing that some inkling of what his father would do in such a situation might be conveyed to him just by being here.

He did not doubt that his mother and father would be delighted that a bride had been found. They would not mind one bit that Miss Spencer's father was not of the nobility. He was rich enough to offer a handsome dowry, and the match was one that would bring together two very powerful enterprises. And like him, they had held very low hopes of such a thing ever coming to pass.

The only problem Everton could see, was that Mr. Spencer was rumored to want his daughter to wed someone with a title. Miss Spencer had certainly, up until her meeting with Henry at least, seemed to show a tendency towards the sons of dukes, marquesses and earls. Bertie had clearly been her favored choice – an earl in his own right, and heir to the Marquess of Kent. He was wealthy, handsome and a good man. No woman in her right mind would ever choose Henry, an untitled second son, over someone with Bertie's pedigree.

But whether he was accepted or not, it had to be seen that Henry was willing to do the right thing. And so, tomorrow, just before lunch, Henry would be on Miss Spencer's doorstep, ready to ask for her hand – whether either of them wished for it or not. And at lunch, he would be at the Forteus Club, where he would buy Bertie Wilson a fine meal and would beg his old friend's forgiveness.

Everton took another sip of the rich port and savored it for a moment before swallowing, then got up and made his way downstairs to the butler's small office. Kingsley was sat at his fire, wire-rimmed spectacles perched upon his nose, entirely engrossed in the book he read. Everton rapped on the glass of the door and cleared his throat politely, to announce himself. He smiled as the elderly butler carefully marked his place in the book with a thin strip of leather, then looked up.

"Master Everton, I am sorry. I did not realize it was you," he said when he saw who was calling upon him at this late hour. He jumped to his feet and stood ramrod straight.

"There is no need to be so formal," Everton said with a smile. "These should be the hours when you may relax." Kingsley gave him an awkward smile but did not relax his posture. He was a fine butler, and he had managed the Cormick household with precision and dedication for over twenty years. Everton handed him the letters he'd penned earlier. "Could you see that these are delivered immediately. I know it is late, but I should like them to be the first things that Lord Wilson and Miss Knorr see in the morning, if you would not mind?"

"I think one of the stable lads is still up," Kingsley said primly. "I shall send him post haste."

Everton smiled and left the old man to his book and his fire. There would be much to be done in the coming days. He wondered briefly as he made his way up the back stairs to the second floor, what Miss Knorr would make of everything that had occurred. She would no doubt be delighted that a match had been made – if Miss Spencer would agree to it. Lady Gertrude had told him that Miss Knorr did not particularly enjoy her new position and of her longing to return to her home near Exeter.

He couldn't help imagining what London would be like without her. The two of them had shared a number of interesting conversations in recent weeks and he had come to look forward to seeing her at the many events around London. She was a breath of fresh air, in so many ways. She was candid and articulate, witty and intelligent. She spoke of the things that mattered, rather than making small talk. Like Lady Gertrude, she was always herself. He admired her for that. In an era when a woman's worth was decided by her beauty, her wealth and her place in Society, Miss Knorr was unbothered by such things. Yet, still managed to live within the constraints Society had set in place – unlike Miss Spencer and Henry, who seemed unconcerned by them and so ignored them.

She was not, of course, here to find a husband as the other girls were. From what he had learned of her past, mostly from Lady Gertrude, Miss Knorr had not found a

match when she Came Out into Devon Society, eight
years previously, though Everton did not know why such
a charming and accomplished young lady would have
struggled to find a suitable husband. He could only
assume that the young men of the surrounding counties
were all fools for letting someone so sweet and good get
away.

He knew that Miss Knorr had never had a London
Season of her own, as her family could not afford such a
thing. It was a very expensive enterprise to launch a
young lady into Society, few families could truly afford to
do so, so that was no shame. Many took the gamble that a
good match would solve all their concerns, but it seemed
that Miss Knorr's family had chosen not to put the pressure on her to save the family's position. And so, she had
only ever acted as a companion to those that did come to
London to try their luck.

Yet she seemed unconcerned about her position. She
knew most young women of her age would be desperate
to find someone to wed, so they might have children and
a household of their own to run. But Miss Knorr never
spoke of such things. That did not mean she did not think
on them, of course. Everton was wise enough to know
that all women had their secrets. But she did not display
any signs of the panic he so often saw in young women
who had not yet married by her age.

He shook his head, as if trying to get rid of such
thoughts, as he opened the doorway onto the second floor
and made his way along the wide, carpeted corridor to his
bed chamber. As he entered the richly decorated rooms,
he could see that his valet had laid out a clean night shirt

on the vast four-poster bed and that there was a steaming jug of water on the washstand. Jenkins was discreet, but he was always watching and seemed to constantly anticipate Everton's every need. Sometimes, Everton tried to catch the young man out – but he never managed to do so.

Everton readied himself for bed, and as he always did before he turned out the lamps, he glanced at the miniature of Katherine on the bedside table. He pressed a kiss to his fingers, then to her lips. "If only you were still here, dearest one," he said to her image as he plumped his pillow and settled himself under the blankets. "You could tell me what to do. Am I making a terrible mistake with Henry? Am I right to push him to proposing to Miss Spencer, or would it be better to ride out the scandal?"

He blew out the lamp and stared up at the ceiling. For the first time since her passing, Katherine did not come to him, not even in his imagination. Instead, it was the flushed cheeks and gentle smile of Miss Knorr that came to mind once more. He tried to conjure Katherine, but he could not. She had left him. He no longer heard her voice in his head and no longer recalled the scent of her hair. He would never forget her. He would not let himself forget her. With a pang of regret for her loss, he suddenly knew that it was time to let her rest in peace, to stop begging her to remain with him in spirit – to let her go. She would not wish for him to waste his days pining for her. She would wish for him to be happy. As he closed his eyes, he couldn't help thinking that she would have liked Miss Knorr. The pair were, in many ways, very alike.

CHAPTER NINE

Anne was not surprised to see another letter by her table setting as she sat down for breakfast. The handwriting was unfamiliar, but she had received missives from all manner of people in the past few days. She slid a knife under the seal and unfolded the thick paper and began to read, an unexpected and gentle smile curving her lips as she did so. She had so come to dread everything in the past few days. It was a pleasure to receive something from someone who seemed to want to help rather than condemn.

Caroline appeared a few moments later, sliding into her seat and accepting a coddled egg and some bread and butter from the footman in attendance. She poured herself a cup of steaming hot chocolate and wrapped her long fingers around the cup. "Is that from your father?" she asked.

"No, it is from Mr. Cormick," Anne said, still a little surprised by it. "He writes to ask for an audience with us, with you, for him and his brother this morning at eleven o'clock."

"Oh, do say yes," Caroline enthused. "I would be delighted to continue my conversation with Henry."

Anne frowned. It was as if Caroline had completely forgotten the feeling of censure and being judged they had experienced at last night's card party. The mere mention of Henry brought a genuine smile to her face. She truly was delighted. "I would imagine they wish to come to discuss what is to be done about the predicament we find ourselves in, not for you to continue to discuss things with Henry Cormick."

"What predicament?" Caroline said, genuinely taken aback. "Lord Wilson was perfectly charming last night. He did not seem in the slightest bit put out. What is there to talk about in regard to a scandal that is no real scandal at all?"

"Are you truly so naïve?" Anne asked. "You think that just because Lord Wilson joined our table at cards last night that everything will be forgotten?"

"Well, it should be," Caroline said pouting a little at being scolded. "Who have we hurt? All we did was talk. Lord Wilson does not seem to mind – and he is the only person who might be of a mind to mind." She paused at the repetition, seeming almost mesmerized by it.

"Lord Wilson has impeccable manners. He would not ever be rude to a lady in public. He did what he did, to save his own face – not to protect yours. However, I do not doubt that he is upset and even if he is not, most of Society is angry on his behalf. Some form of action will be required – and it is up to us to find a way to placate

Society's outrage so that your prospects are not permanently tarnished."

"So, how do I put that right?" Caroline said. "I can hardly be held responsible for the good humor of the entirety of *the Ton*."

"I am not sure," Anne said. "But hopefully, Mr. Cormick will have some idea of how we might rectify matters when he arrives."

Caroline glanced up at the clock. It was almost ten o'clock now. She blanched a little and pushed her plate away. "I shall have to hurry to dress," she said and got up and ran out of the room.

Anne set the letter down and ate her breakfast, alone in the silent dining room. She pondered over what might be done. Last night's card party had confirmed to her that Society would continue to judge Caroline and Henry until they saw, to their satisfaction, that something had been done. The only thing that Anne could think of that might help was a betrothal – and that seemed unlikely. Henry Cormick did not seem to her to be the kind of man that really wished to be wed.

Her meal finished, Anne went upstairs and checked on Caroline. Her lady's maid was carefully curling and pinning her hair, and Caroline had chosen a sprigged muslin gown that flattered her well. Anne did not doubt it had been selected by her lady's maid, as Caroline had no concept of what suited her or not.

With a heavy sigh, Anne moved on to her own room, where she picked out a green satin dress and then carefully fixed her own hair, before she made her way along the corridor to Mrs. Spencer's suite. Everyone in the house knew better than to disturb the older woman until well past half past ten, and Anne arrived as Maisie, one of the chamber maids, was knocking upon Mrs. Spencer's door, with her pot of morning chocolate.

"I'll take that," Anne said, as Maisie handed her the tray.

"Enter," Mrs. Spencer called out. Anne opened the door and went inside. Mrs. Spencer was propped up in her bed, a frilled dressing gown fastened tightly around her plump body. "Ah, Miss Knorr, how lovely. How was last night?"

"Not good," Anne admitted as she settled the tray on Mrs. Spencer's lap and took a seat by the side of the bed. "And I do not think that Caroline fully understands the precariousness of the situation."

"I feared something like this might happen," Mrs. Spencer said with a sigh. "She is so willful, and it is so hard for her to pretend otherwise."

Anne nodded her agreement. "However," she said, handing over the note that Mr. Cormick had sent her, "there may be hope of a resolution."

Mrs. Spencer read slowly, running her finger under each word and mouthing them silently. "Do you think this is a good thing?" she said finally, having reached Mr. Cormick's signature.

"I do. Mr. Cormick is a highly respected young man. He is clever and understands *the Ton*, he is very much a part of the highest echelons of Society. I don't doubt he will have a solution."

"Do you need me to be present?" Mrs. Spencer asked a little anxiously. "I fear I may not know what to say. I was not brought up in this world, after all. I don't really understand it. It affects my nerves most terribly, all of this."

"No, you may rest here," Anne assured her. "I know that this matter has played on your mind greatly. I shall come up and tell you everything immediately they leave."

"Oh, thank you, Anne. I know I was cross with you the other day, but I truly do not know what we would do without you." Anne gave the older lady's hand a gentle squeeze then headed downstairs. She wasn't so sure that she was the right person to deal with all of this, either, but someone had to ensure that Caroline's reputation was not lost due to such a silly mishap.

Both young women were seated, a little nervously, in the drawing room, when a loud knock on the door announced their guests. Caroline almost jumped out of her skin. Anne felt a jumble of snakes in the pit of her stomach begin to writhe and hiss. Contrarily to the two young women's nerves, Mr. Cormick strode confidently into the room behind Mrs. Graham, the housekeeper, with Henry trailing behind as usual. Polite greetings were exchanged as a maid brought a silver tray with a coffee pot and cups upon it. Anne offered to pour, glad of the opportunity to do something, though she had to disguise an uncharacteristic shake to her hands as she did so.

She handed a cup to Henry first, who took it and immediately moved to sit beside Caroline. The pair looked at one another for a moment, then launched into conversation as if they had never been apart. Anne shook her head as she poured another cup for Mr. Cormick. She handed it to him, her hand shaking a little. His fingers brushed hers, ever so slightly, as she did so. Anne felt a shiver of sensation flood over her, and the heat of a blush rise up from her chest into her cheeks. She turned away and poured a cup for herself, taking a couple of deep breaths to calm herself.

When she turned back, he had taken the armchair by the window and was sat comfortably sipping at his drink. Anne took the sofa beside him and perched on the edge of the seat as she took a first sip of the dark, bitter liquid. "I was glad to receive your letter," she said nervously.

"I did not know if it would be best to write to you first, or to Miss Spencer's Mama," Mr. Cormick said quietly. "I hope I did not make the wrong choice."

"No, not at all. Mrs. Spencer is glad that you wrote to me. She is indisposed this morning."

"Then I am glad I made the choice that I did." He glanced over at Caroline and Henry who were engaged in passionate discussion already. "So, we must find a way to put things right, to protect Miss Spencer's reputation – and salvage a little of Lord Wilson's pride, if we may."

"Indeed, though I am not sure how we might do such a thing," Anne admitted.

"There is a way," Mr. Cormick said cautiously. "But it is rather drastic."

"Marriage?"

"You thought that, too," he said with a grin. "I should have known that you would already have considered it."

"But would Henry be willing?" she asked.

"He seems to be. Would Caroline mind such a match?"

"I don't think so. She said to me that she longed for

someone like Henry, someone she could be herself with. Whether or not her father would agree, well, that is another matter. He has it in mind that his daughter and grandchild might have a title, to cement the family's place in Society."

"Does he not know that these days such draconian measures are not required," Mr. Cormick said with a grin. Anne smiled at his attempt at levity. "After all, am I not at the very epitome of Society? I have no title, but my family are good friends with Prinny, and my father was a good friend to Beau Brummel in the day."

"Your mother does have noble blood though, does she not?" Anne enquired, recalling something that Lady Gertrude had once told her about the Cormick's heritage.

"She does, but there are many in Society now that do not." He paused. "Do you truly think that there might be an issue with Mr. Spencer granting his consent?"

Anne nodded. "I do. I wish I did not, because it is by far the most sensible solution to the matter at hand. But because Mr. and Mrs. Spencer did not grow up in Society, they do not always understand those peculiar unwritten rules regarding the protection of a young woman's honor."

"Then we need to convince Mr. Spencer of the merits of such a thing," Mr. Cormick said as if it would be the simplest thing in the world.

"Convince me of the merits of what, exactly," a booming voice said, as Mr. Spencer appeared in the doorway of the drawing room, his travelling clothes covered in dust from the long journey. Everyone jumped to their feet as he removed his coat, hat and gloves and handed them to a nearby footman. Mr. Cormick and Henry bowed respectfully, Anne and Caroline curtseyed deeply.

Caroline rushed to her father's side and reached up to press a kiss on his fleshy cheek. He beamed at her. "I thought I was here to have some young fool ask for your hand."

"You are, Papa," Caroline said a little nervously as she tucked her arm through her father's and led him to the sofa. He sat down heavily. "Just not the man Mama wrote to you about."

Mr. Spencer looked a little confused. "Your mother said there was an earl sniffing around you, don't tell me that you've gone and upset him somehow."

Caroline blushed and sat down beside her father, holding his hand tightly. "Please don't be angry with me, but I may have..." she broke off and looked plaintively at Anne.

"What Caroline is trying to say, sir," Anne said, trying her best to sound confident and assured, "is that there has been a little misunderstanding."

"What kind of misunderstanding?" Mr. Spencer roared at her, his face turning redder by the moment. He turned back to his daughter. "Don't tell me you've let some penniless fool tup you on a terrace somewhere."

"Nothing like that, sir," Anne assured him. "But there was an incident at Almack's the other evening. Miss Caroline and Mr. Cormick, here," she pointed to Henry, "got talking and were so taken up by their conversation that Miss Spencer missed all of the dances."

Mr. Spencer looked a little confused. "I don't see why

talking with someone is a problem," he said. "Not like she was up to something behind anyone's back, is it?"

"No, but Society tends to become more than a little put out by such things," Mr. Cormick tried to explain. "A young woman's honor and virtue are most precious, and there are many ways in which a young woman might lose them. Unfortunately, being seen to favor one-man over all others – when not affianced to that man – is one of them."

"Nonsense," Mr. Spencer spluttered, then he paused looking at his daughter and Henry Cormick, then at Anne and Mr. Cormick. "So, talking to this young whippersnapper has ruined my girl?" He nodded towards Henry.

"Something like that, sir," Henry said looking shamefaced. "I must assure you that I did not intend for such a thing to happen and will do whatever is in my power to put it right."

"And you are?" Mr. Spencer asked.

"Henry, sir. Henry Cormick." Henry bowed again, dipping his tousled head low.

"And you are not an earl," Mr. Spencer said simply.

"No, sir. I am not. I am the second son of Wilfred Cormick. You may have heard of him. He is a very successful man."

"I know of him," Mr. Spencer said narrowing his eyes as he looked Henry over, clearly thinking of the advantages such a match might bring his own interests. "A fine man of business, and one I'd like to get to know in person. Such an introduction could be beneficial to us both." He paused. "Only a second son, though. And no title."

Anne cringed at how gauche Mr. Spencer was being. She barely dared to glance at Mr. Cormick to see how he was reacting to what was being said. When she did, she could see that he was struggling to contain his anger at his brother being dismissed out of hand by such a man as Mr. Spencer. "Sir," he said. "I do not think you quite grasp the situation. If you do not permit Miss Spencer to marry my brother, then it may well be that no man in Society will consider her. It is a harsh fate, but one I have seen happen all too often. Once a young woman's honor is gone, it is almost impossible for her to regain her place amongst *the Ton*."

"It is true," Anne urged. "Even if Lord Wilson still cares for Miss Spencer, he would never be able to marry her now – and neither would anyone else."

Mr. Spencer tapped his thick fingers on his breeches impatiently and mugged a little as their words sank in. "And your income young man, what of that?" he asked, turning back to Henry.

"Currently, ten thousand pounds a year," Henry said quickly. "But my father assured me that should I marry, it would be increased to fifteen thousand pounds."

"Not much, but with Caroline's dowry, it would make things comfortable enough for you," Mr. Spencer mused. "How about property?"

"Nothing of my own, but the family owns an estate in Hertfordshire, and a townhouse in Mayfair. There is also a hunting lodge in Scotland."

At the mention of an estate and a hunting lodge, Mr. Spencer looked a little more pleased at the prospect of letting his daughter wed someone without a title. "But no title? No noble blood?" He turned to Mr. Cormick. "And I presume everything comes to you as the first son?"

"My father has made generous provision for Henry in his will," Mr. Cormick assured him. "And our mother is the daughter of an earl. As a family, we are blessed to count the Prince Regent as a family friend and have been invited to his coronation at the end of the Season." This was no small matter, as only a very select group had been invited to attend the actual coronation itself. It bestowed great esteem upon the Cormicks and cemented their position in the highest echelon of *the Ton*.

And the information had done what it needed to. Mr. Spencer was beginning to look almost happy at the idea of a match with such a family. Anne gave Mr. Cormick a brief smile. What a wonderful thing to be able to boast. It was just the type of thing that might appeal to a man such as this. Mr. Spencer looked at his daughter. "And what of you, you silly ninny?" he asked her. "Are you happy to marry to get yourself out of this mess?"

"Oh, Papa," Caroline sighed, glancing over at Henry with an uncharacteristically soppy expression. "I am."

"Then I suppose there will be a wedding," Mr. Spencer said with a shrug. Caroline immediately covered his face in kisses and then bounced over to where Henry was standing, still looking a little bewildered by everything that had just occurred. "I'll see the vicar later today to get the banns read immediately. I'd like to get it done as soon as possible so I can return to my work."

CHAPTER TEN

"Well, that wasn't how I imagined such a thing would likely go," Henry joked nervously, showing uncharacteristic anxiety, as the brother's got into their carriage and made their way to the Forteus Club to meet with Bertie Wilson. "I don't think I've ever been so concerned that a thing might not come off." Everton smiled, but he too had begun to think that their arguments just might not work to convince the rather intransigent Mr. Spencer. But things had gone about as well as could possibly have been expected. Everton could only hope that this next *rendez-vous* would be as successful as the one they had just left.

"I must confess, I had always thought such a thing – even with you - would be at least a little bit more romantic," Everton said to his brother with a shake of his head and a wry grin. "I remember when I asked for Katherine's hand, things were considerably easier."

"He really did want a title, didn't he?" Henry

marveled. "I've never really understood the desire for one myself. Everyone I know who has one wishes they didn't."

"It can be a burden," Everton agreed. "Carrying the weight of expectation of generations." He thought about how hard his dear friends, Claveston St. John and William Pierce, had struggled to come to terms with the lives they had been destined to lead from before they were even born. To be the son of a nobleman was a heavy burden for some. They had both struggled but had come out on the other side – happily wed and content with their futures.

The brothers were quiet for a few minutes, both lost in their thoughts, as the carriage trundled through the streets from Kensington towards Bond Street, where the Forteus Club welcomed its exclusive clientele. Everton came rarely, but Henry attended most days when he was in London. He was greeted warmly by everyone, probably because he owed so many of them money. "You will do something about your gambling, won't you, once you're married?" Everton whispered as they walked through the marble hallway, with its vast staircase and many busts of previous members of specific importance and went into the main attending room.

The room was a complete contrast from the perfectly white marble in the entrance hallway. It was dark, the walls were wood-paneled and lined with bookshelves filled with leather-bound books tooled with gold leaf. The rich mahogany furniture and leather armchairs gave the place a very masculine feel. No woman had ever passed the doors of the club in its hundred- and fifty-year history. Perhaps that was why Everton did not enjoy it that much. He enjoyed the company of women, unlike Henry who had never shown much interest in them – until recently, at least.

"I gamble whilst in London because I am often bored," Henry admitted as they took a seat at their usual table by the fire. "There is little to do here during the Season, and you know how much I struggle in company. Playing cards does not require much conversation. Even I can manage it without making some terrible gaffe – like I did at Almack's with Miss Spencer. I am not made for the life of *the Ton*. I cannot do small talk. I need real things to talk about. Even working for Father is preferable than this life of forced indolence. At least one has something to do."

Everton couldn't help being amused. It was well known throughout their father's enterprises just how little Henry liked any of the work he had been set to over the years. Though he and Father had tried their best to find a niche that suited Henry, it had been to no avail so far. "And you think that you will find sufficient conversation in a marriage to Miss Spencer?"

"You know, I do," Henry said cheerfully. "She doesn't much like people, either – but we both love logic and exploring the things that bore most others."

Everton remembered the conversation he'd had with Miss Knorr about Henry's love of the academic life. "Would you like me to speak with Father," Everton asked, curious as to what Henry might answer, "about your returning to university, pursuing a career there, I mean?"

"No, I understand that there is only so far that a man can push his luck," Henry said with a wry chuckle. "I shall be glad I've found a wife that they will be happy with – that I will be happy with – for now." But his eyes had lit up at just the mention of such a possibility. Everton decided that he would indeed make enquiries on his brother's behalf.

His thoughts, and their conversation, were interrupted by the arrival of Lord Bertie Wilson, who plopped himself down unceremoniously in the chair opposite Everton. It was hard to believe that such a puppy of a man would one day be a Marquess, and that he was heir to one of the richest and oldest estates in the land. "How the devil are you both?" he asked, as jovial as ever. Everton couldn't help but marvel that this was a man that until a day or two ago had presumed himself in love and had been cuckolded in plain view of all of Society.

"We are well," Everton said cautiously, wondering if Bertie was just doing his best to make things easy on everyone else – as he so often had in college. He was always the one attempting to break up the fights, to placate those vehemently opposed to one another. He liked for everyone to get along.

"Then what's all this about? Not like the pair of you to invite me to lunch." Bertie hailed one of the footmen and ordered himself a large brandy. "You two want one?" he asked them. It surprised Everton that even Bertie should be so unaware as to why the Cormicks might wish to meet with him.

"A bottle of claret might be more suitable to go with lunch, don't you think, old man?" Everton said.

Bertie shook his head and laughed. "Of course, you're right – as always. Claret it is. And chops all round?"

The brothers nodded their assent. The club wasn't renowned for its fine dining, but the chops were always cooked well and had good flavor. The footman disappeared and Bertie looked at them both expectantly. Henry looked first at Everton, then at Bertie and took a deep breath. He leaned forward in his chair. "Thing is, old man," he started a little nervously, "the thing is, I've asked Miss Spencer for her hand."

"You have?" Bertie said, gulping a little as if trying to swallow his disappointment, but then beaming, as ever, determined to do the right thing. "Capital news. Delighted for you both. Must confess, I'm not surprised. The pair of you were thick as thieves at Almack's. Made for each other, you might say."

For all his bluster, Bertie was a genuinely decent man. Everton gave him a supportive smile. "I know you had hopes yourself," he said gently.

"Yes, well. Not the first time I've been pipped at the post, eh, lads? Remember that race we had, second year at Oxford, I was so close to beating Ponty Bevan."

"Yes, you were. The whole college yelled themselves hoarse for you," Henry said, then added in a soft voice, "I do care for her. I'll make her happy."

"I know you will. She's too clever for a chap like me, knew that from the start. But she seemed not to mind that I'm not all that. Still, plenty of fillies in town, bound to find someone, right?"

"Bound to," the brothers echoed.

"You're quite a catch, after all. They were queuing up for you, I'm sure they will again," Everton added.

"You know, I'm glad you sorted things," Bertie said to Henry, his big blue eyes earnest and a little sad. "I was dreading having to call you out – but I would have done, if you'd not done the right thing by her."

"Then it is as well that all has ended well," Henry said. "You know I'm hopeless at anything like that."

"Yes, that was precisely why I dreaded it." They all laughed at Bertie's very weak joke. Such matters demanded satisfaction, but that meant that good friends could find themselves at odds – and at the end of a pistol. It was a blessing that this time such a thing was not required.

The rest of the luncheon passed amicably. The three old friends joked and laughed together, sharing stories of Henry and Bertie's time at Oxford and the scrapes they'd gotten into. The trio parted late in the afternoon, vowing to get together again soon. "He really is a capital fellow," Henry said as they drove home. "Just as well it was him and not someone else."

Everton didn't say anything but couldn't help agreeing. Almost anyone else of their acquaintance would have called out the duel that very night. They certainly wouldn't have delayed for two days as Bertie had. Henry had been very lucky indeed to escape unharmed. But Bertie was loyal and sweet, and though an excellent shot and a champion boxer in his day, he was not the kind to engage in violence unless absolutely necessary. Everton didn't doubt that Bertie was as relieved at the outcome of the affair as he himself was.

"Your Miss Knorr is rather spectacular, isn't she," Henry said suddenly.

"Hardly my Miss Knorr," he protested. He respected Miss Knorr immensely, and was glad of her friendship, but there truly was nothing more to it than that.

Henry shook his head. "You know what I mean. You were the one that introduced me to her, and you and she made an excellent team back there - with Mr. Spencer, I mean."

"Oh," Everton said, a little relieved. "Yes, she is a remarkable woman."

"You were trying to push us together at first, weren't you?"

"Unusually perceptive of you, brother."

"I have my moments," Henry said grinning. "I could have been happy with her, I think. But I doubt she would have been so content with me."

Such introspection was unusual from Henry. It rather took Everton aback. "What do you mean by that?"

"Miss Knorr is clever and sweet, kind and very witty. But she is also quiet and studious. Those aspects of her would have suited me very well."

"But?"

"But she is like you. She likes people. Not to see and be seen, but she genuinely likes people. She'd want to have guests and family to stay all the time. She'd expect me to be sociable and would want to dance and play duets. I'd hate that."

Everton laughed. It was so like Henry to think of the

imposition to his personal choices that a wife would make. "Do you not think that Miss Spencer might be the same? She has danced more than Miss Knorr and played the pianoforte more often when we have been in company."

"She'd give it all up tomorrow, she told me," Henry explained. "She does everything she does because she knows it is what is expected. I told her she need not ever expect to have to do anything she does not enjoy once we are married."

"And you intend for her to give you permission to do the same?" Everton raised an eyebrow quizzically. His experience, limited thought it was, with women was that they inevitably had an agenda of their own. Happiness in a marriage seemed to depend upon how closely matched a pair's intentions were in the first place.

"I do. But you make it sound like it is a bad thing. We both like studying, are happiest when buried in a library of books – and we love to discuss our findings. I think we will find one another excellent companions in that sense. You know, she is the only person I have found, outside of my college professors, that I can truly be myself with. She likes me as I am. And I like her. Many might see her as cold, too clever for a woman, but that is to her credit, I think."

Everton flexed his fingers and leant back against the walls of the coach. Perhaps Henry was right. Perhaps they were perfectly matched. But he couldn't help thinking that Henry was overlooking a major flaw in his own future happiness. His brother hated working for their father. He could tolerate it for now, but in time he would grow fractious and impatient. He would rant and rail, and make both his own life, and that of his wife, a misery. He vowed to speak with their father about it, whether Henry wished it or not. There had to be a way to use Henry's particular skills in a way that would make his brother happy and benefit the family somehow. When Henry realized the whirl of engagements that would be expected of him in the run up to his wedding, he would need something to look forward to.

Their parents did not delay their arrival in London following their receipt of Everton's letter telling them the good news. Within two days they had arrived from Hertfordshire. Mama swept into the house as if she were a queen, beaming with delight. She covered both her sons' faces with kisses, then insisted they tell her everything about Henry's betrothed. They all took their seats in the drawing room, and the two brothers told their parents' the entire sorry saga of what had happened. Everton had expected them to be a little disappointed in Henry, but it seemed that they were both too delighted that he had actually found a bride to mind how he had gone about it.

"When will we meet her?" she asked impatiently when it was clear that a description of Miss Spencer was not going to be enough.

"She will be at Lady Grey's musicale tonight," Henry assured his mother. "You will meet her then."

"And is there anyone that has taken your eye?" she asked Everton hopefully.

Everton squeezed her hand. "I'm not yet ready," he told her. "But I am making progress."

She smiled at him and kissed his cheek. "I am glad to

hear that. Katherine would want you to look for love again, I am sure of it. She had so much of it to give. She would not wish for you to live without it." She stood up and caressed both men's cheeks. "Now, if I am to meet my future daughter-in-law, then I will retire for a nap, so I am rested and at my best for tonight's entertainment."

CHAPTER ELEVEN

Caroline was actually nervous. Anne couldn't quite believe what she was witnessing, as she watched the young woman anxiously rifling through her best gowns, taking them out of the armoire one after the other, then discarding them with a loud tut. She then began the same process with her jewelry box, trying to find the perfect combination for her presentation that evening to Mrs. Cormick. She had never seen the young woman so ill at ease, so unsure of herself.

"Anne, she was brought up in one of the finest households in the country," Caroline moaned, sinking on to the bed and burying her face in her hands, still undecided upon how to present herself at this evening's musicale. "If I offend her tonight, she may never grow to like me. She might even put a stop to the match, and I couldn't bear that. Henry is the only person I have ever known who actually likes me."

It was so sad to hear such a beautiful girl say such things. She should have had the world at her feet, given her wealth and beauty - yet she was right. There was something about her that made many people feel awkward around her. She did not mean to be unkind. She longed to be liked. Yet she seemed destined to offend with her bluntness and inability to lie, even the tiniest of white lies. Caroline was an enigma, yet she was also a completely open book – and that frightened many in Society, where the rules of behavior and decorum had stood the test of time for generations. Caroline challenged everything they had ever known.

"And she will be delighted by you, whatever you wear," Anne assured her gently, "because you wish to marry her son." She paused, trying to think of what might placate her young charge, and put her overly anxious mind at ease. Caroline was such an unusual girl. She was at times utterly aloof, and yet was so alert to criticism that she tried too hard to please. With Mary, or even with Lady Gertrude any number of common platitudes would work in a situation like this. But Caroline needed whatever was said to her to be irrefutably true so she could not disregard it.

Anne couldn't stop the image of Mr. Everton Cormick pushing into her head unbidden, his warm smile and gentle ways. He was always so considerate, so thoughtful. He made sure that she danced at every ball and had someone to escort her to supper. He would have willingly escorted Anne and Caroline home, Anne was sure of that, if Caroline hadn't usually been previously accounted for. And Henry, well he was an unusual sort, but he was keenly attuned to what was fair and right, though he was not always the most sociable of men. Yet, he did his best to behave as Society insisted was right. They were unusually kind, straightforward people in a sea of false impressions and fake amity.

"Think upon what good, kind people both Mr. Cormick and your Henry are," Anne said eventually. "They would not be that way if they had not been raised so beautifully by their Mama," she said moving towards the bed and starting to sort through the chaos Caroline had left in her wake.

Caroline sighed heavily. "I know that you are right. But I so wish to make a good impression upon Henry's family. I know I am not good with people. It is so hard for me. I watch the other girls as they giggle and flirt and gossip. It's is so easy for them. I have to force myself to even smile and to bite my tongue whenever someone nearby says something inane."

"I know," Anne said. "And yet you have done so with aplomb for weeks. Just a few more, and you will be wed, and in the country where you can be yourself. After all, Henry has assured you that he wants nothing more than for you to be yourself."

Anne picked through the pile of gowns now thrown over the bed, hanging them carefully back in the armoire so they would not crease, and pulled out a wine-red silk that would be perfect for the evening. There were not many blondes that could pull off such bold, rich colors, but Caroline was one of the exceptions. Being pale was the trend, but Caroline's golden tan never faded no matter how much she remained indoors and so she could be bolder with the colors she chose as they would not wash her out.

"I think this one," Anne said nodding to herself as she held it up to Caroline.

The young woman looked a little surprised at Anne's choice. "You do not think it too much? That something more dainty, pretty – girlish even – might not be a better choice?"

"Caroline, I think it is about time that you accepted yourself, as you are," Anne said firmly. "You are not a prim parlor miss. You never will be. You have tried hard to fit that mold, but it has made you most unhappy. You are soon to be wed to a man who would never be content with such a woman anyway. He has chosen you because you are unlike every other girl in Society."

"But did he really choose me?" Caroline wailed, cradling her lovely face in her hands and rocking slowly back and forth. Her fears truly had taken a very strong hold over her usually very sensible mind. "He was forced into his proposal, after all."

"I do not believe that Henry Cormick would ever have agreed to wed anyone if he thought that doing so was not precisely what he wanted."

"You do know him well, I suppose," Caroline mused, but she did not sound convinced. "But just because Henry is prepared to accept me, does not mean that his family will. Mr. Cormick does not like me at all, I can tell."

Anne gave a wry chuckle. "He simply does not know what to make of you," she said. "He likes you well enough to be your brother-in-law. He certainly fought hard to make you a part of his family."

Thankfully, the maids appeared with the copper

bathtub and pails of hot water for Caroline's ablutions at that moment and Anne was spared any further panic as Caroline submerged herself in the tub and Anne went to wash and dress herself. She was feeling a little nervous herself, unsure if it was because it was so important to Caroline, or because she would be seeing Mr. Cormick once more. She kept thinking of that moment when their hands had touched. An innocent enough brush of skin against skin, yet it had left such a vivid impression upon Anne's imagination. The shiver of anticipation, the quiver of unexpected desire – something she had never before felt for any man – had profoundly shocked and delighted her.

He was such a good man. He seemed to genuinely care for the people in his life, and she longed to be included amongst that number. He was already solicitous and seemed genuinely interested in her thoughts, and always sought her out to dance. It made her feel special, in a way she had never before known. Yet he seemed to show no interest at all in anyone else, except perhaps Lady Gertrude. Anne knew her position in Society was one of tolerance. As a companion she had no real status at all. Lady Gertrude would be a perfect match for Mr. Cormick – and what a handsome couple they would make, too. Yet, despite knowing it to be impossible, secretly Anne wished that he might truly notice her.

She dressed carefully for the evening's entertainment. There was much at stake and even a lowly companion's attire and comportment might affect the outcome. It would not only be the first time that Caroline would meet her future parents-in-law, but the first time that the Cormicks would meet Mr. and Mrs. Spencer. Anne was no fool, she knew that it would be very likely that it would fall upon her to smooth out any difficulties that might occur. Mrs. Spencer could be counted upon to at least be silent if she felt ill at ease amongst company – and had grown somewhat used to the mores of Society during their weekly At Home. But Anne feared for Mr. Spencer. His bluff and oftentimes brash approach would no doubt make hackles rise. Given how much this match mattered to Caroline, Anne was determined to do all she could to ensure nothing stood in its way.

As the grandfather clock in the hallway struck seven o'clock, Anne and Caroline made their way downstairs. Mrs. Spencer was already waiting for them, her cloak and hat already on. She looked nervous, and Anne was certain that underneath her pretty lace gloves there would be nails bitten to the quick. "Oh, my dears, you both look lovely," she cooed as they approached her. Her husband emerged from his study. "Don't they look lovely, Mr. Spencer?" she added as Anne and Caroline took their evening cloaks from Caroline's lady's maid and put them on.

Mr. Spencer rolled his eyes and grunted. His wife glared at him. "I'm sure, I'm sure," he said hurriedly, buttoning his jacket over his vast belly and reaching for his coat. "Let's get this over with." He grabbed a silver-topped cane from the stand that stood by the door and set his top hat on his head, then ushered them all out into the cool night air.

The carriage ride passed without anyone speaking, though Mr. Spencer's heavy breathing and occasional grunts meant it was certainly not in silence. With every particularly loud noise, Mrs. Spencer seemed to grow more nervous, as if she feared that her husband might embarrass them all. But as they pulled up outside Lady Grey's fine mansion, he pulled himself up straighter and seemed to transform before their very eyes. He got out of the coach first, then gallantly offered his hand to his wife, then his daughter, and finally to Anne. He beamed, which rather took them all aback, as he so rarely did anything other than scowl.

A footman took his coat and the ladies' cloaks, and the butler took them to a large ballroom filled with chairs in neat rows, with people milling around and talking in huddled groups, and announced them. Nobody seemed to be paying any attention to the new arrivals, so they made their way inside and accepted the offer of a cup of fruit punch from one of the servants as they waited for someone of their acquaintance to approach them.

Lady Gertrude, thankfully, arrived just a few moments after them and as soon as she saw them, made straight for the corner where they stood. She greeted Caroline and Mrs. Spencer warmly and seemed to even charm Mr. Spencer with her intelligent questions about his business affairs. "You know a lot for such a pretty young thing," he complimented her.

"My father has never seen fit to think that conversation about business should be kept from the dinner table," Lady Gertrude informed him with a smile. "I grew up knowing far more than I should."

"Perhaps I should have done that more myself," Mr. Spencer said. "My Caro's got a sharp mind. She'd probably understand it all better than any of my overseers and clerks."

Caroline flushed at the compliment, though Anne wasn't entirely sure if she was pleased by it or was bristling at an old slight. True, such a remark wasn't the kind most girls would have wished to receive, but Anne could imagine a younger Caroline begging her father to let her learn at his side. "I'd be honored to learn now," Caroline informed her father, and he nodded resignedly. Anne's suspicions suddenly seemed much more likely, that this was an old family war – one that Mr. Spencer may eventually have to accept defeat in one day. "I think I'd much prefer looking at ledgers than persisting with embroidery," Caroline added. Everyone laughed. Caroline might be accomplished in many areas, but the delicacy of needlework evaded her usually quick mind, and meant she was tormented by a thumb covered in pin pricks.

"If your new husband permits, I'd be glad to show you," Mr. Spencer said, giving in much to Caroline's delight.

"I shall convince him of its merits," his daughter assured him.

"I did not have a son," Mr. Spencer said ruefully, "but someone will need to take on the business affairs when I am gone. I would like that person to be of my blood." He looked at his daughter proudly which made Anne smile, too. Suddenly, Caroline's world might be opening to her, offering her tasks and interests she might actually take pleasure in – rather than forcing herself to those that bored her.

But there was no time to dwell upon such things, as the Cormicks had arrived. Henry didn't even wait to greet Lady Grey before he rushed forwards to greet his bride-to-be, a leather folio in his hand. He looked as excited as a young puppy, and she was not much different as he clasped her hand in his and pressed a kiss to the back of it. "I have the score for tonight's sonata, would you care to look it over with me before the performance commences?" he asked, unintentionally ignoring everyone else.

Caroline grinned at him, clearly as eager to rush off as him, but a quick glance at Anne who frowned and nodded towards both sets of parents soon made her pause. "I should, very much," she said laughing, "but I do think you might say good evening to my parents first – and that I should meet yours before we do so."

Henry looked abashed, then grinned puppylike at his bride-to-be. "Of course, of course," he spluttered. "Where are my manners? Mama will be most upset with me for being so remiss." He turned, still holding Caroline's hand. "I am delighted to see you again, Mr. and Mrs. Spencer."

By now, Mr. and Mrs. Cormick and Everton Cormick had approached their little group and were all chuckling at Henry's inept introductions. "I would like to assure you that I did bring him up with better manners," Mrs. Cormick said to Mrs. Spencer and Caroline. A look of confusion passed over her lovely face as she looked at Caroline, but it was replaced quickly with her warm smile once more. "But I fear that when he is excited, he forgets them utterly. I am Elizabeth Cormick." She leaned forward and kissed the air at both sides of Mrs. Spencer's plump cheeks, then did the same to Caroline.

"Harriet Spencer," Mrs. Spencer said softly. "Our Caroline is much the same." She looked a little flushed, as the two women took each other's measure, though it was clear that despite the gulf in their social standing, that the two of them immediately liked one another. "There is only so much one can do as a mother to prepare them for the world, is there not?"

"I think it as well that the two of them found one another," Mrs. Spencer said warmly. "They can be as socially inept together as they like."

"Father, might I introduce you to Mr. Spencer?" Henry said cheerfully, clearly not at all ashamed of the comments about his lack of social graces. The two older men nodded to one another and shook hands firmly.

"Good to meet you, Spencer," Mr. Cormick said. "I've heard much about your enterprises in the north. I'd be interested to learn more. Perhaps we might be of use to one another."

"I'd be delighted," Mr. Spencer said, and genuinely looked it, too. Within moments, the two men had drifted away, in search of some port and a place to discuss business. Mrs. Cormick sighed. "I must apologize," she said with a wry smile. "Business is all that matters to him, sometimes."

CHAPTER TWELVE

The two older women retired to some seats nearby as Caroline and Henry moved into the nearby corner just out of earshot, leaving Miss Knorr, Lady Gertrude, Miss Jessup and Everton standing together. "Good evening to you all," Everton said and bowed to the three young women. They all smiled at him and bobbed demure curtseys. "Well, that went better than I could have possibly hoped," he admitted with relief.

"Did you truly doubt it would?" Lady Gertrude said with a smile. "Your father and Mr. Spencer will find much in common; they are like peas in a pod when it comes to their business interests – and your mother has never been unkind to anyone in her life."

"That is certainly true," Everton agreed as the Duchess of Devonshire arrived to a flurry of excitement in the room. Her Grace glanced around the room and smiled as her eyes landed upon Lady Gertrude. The elegantly attired duchess beckoned her to join her small group.

"Please forgive me, dear Miss Knorr," Lady Gertrude said with a grin, taking Miss Knorr's hands in hers, "but I must attend Lady Elizabeth, if you will excuse me. Perhaps we can speak later?"

"I should like that," Miss Knorr said with a gentle smile. Everton couldn't help thinking how lovely she looked. Her pale skin and rose-flushed cheeks seemed to possess a rather delightful glow tonight. They watched as Lady Gertrude strode towards the duchess, Miss Jessup trailing behind her. "She is quite remarkable, isn't she?" Miss Knorr marveled. "Lady Gertrude, I mean."

"She is definitely a force of something," Everton agreed. "Though Her Grace is also something of a marvel, I always think." Anne nodded, clearly aware of the tales that had been the talk of Europe some years before. Lady Elizabeth had openly lived with the Duke of Devonshire and his first wife for many years, a scandalous situation that had kept the tongues throughout Society wagging for many, many years and probably would continue to do so for generations.

"I must confess," Everton admitted, "that I will be glad when Wycliffe returns from his wedding tour and relieves me of my duties as older brother-by-proxy."

"You dislike escorting Lady Gertrude?" Miss Knorr asked, wide-eyed, obviously surprised he would say such a thing.

"I do not, but I would like to have an evening to myself from time to time," he admitted with a grin. "She has such potential for getting herself into mischief, don't you think? I feel I need eyes in the back of my head."

"I doubt she would do anything to embarrass herself,

her family – or you," Miss Knorr assured him. "She enjoys a little mischief, that is true enough, but there is nothing malicious in her – and she knows how she must behave."

"You are right, of course," Everton agreed. "And it has been due to her friendship with yourself that Henry has found a bride – something I feared would never happen – so I should not be unkind."

They glanced over to the corner of the room, where Caroline and Henry were poring over the manuscript, their usual passionate conversation in full flow. "I cannot think of a pair better suited to one another," Miss Knorr said with an indulgent smile. "I think they may be the happiest pairing here."

Everton couldn't help but agree. His brother had somehow managed to find someone utterly perfect for him. But he was unable to say as much, as their hostess appeared at the front of the room, tapping on her glass for everyone's attention. "Please, ladies and gentlemen, take your seats for tonight's performance," Lady Grey said, welcoming the musicians to the small plinth erected for them. Everyone dutifully began to take their seats.

Everton sat beside his mother. "You could have warned me," she hissed at him before his backside had even reached the seat.

"Of what?" he asked, bemused.

"That Henry's Caroline so resembles Katherine," she said pointedly. "Does that not bother you?"

Everton sighed. "To tell the truth, I had forgotten," he said honestly enough. "I won't lie, when I first saw her, my heart skipped a beat, and I thought my beloved had returned to me. But then we got to know her, and I realized that there was nothing that she and Katherine share – other than their physical appearance."

"Miss Spencer does seem a little unusual," Mama said with a grin. "She and Henry will suit very well from all I have witnessed thus far."

"They truly do," Everton agreed, glancing over at the pair who were still avidly poring over the music and discussing it in rapid whispers. "They've been like this from the first."

"I am glad. I worried about him. He has always been so unlike everyone else," she said lovingly. "But what about you? Have you had any time to yourself, between shepherding Henry and looking out for dear Gertrude?"

"Not much, but I do not mind."

His mother paused and glanced over at Miss Knorr, sat demurely by Caroline Spencer's side. "You seemed to be rather engrossed in your conversation with Miss Spencer's companion." She smiled knowingly.

"We are merely friends, Mama," Everton assured her, but his mother's smile did not fade.

"We'll see," she said as the first notes of the sonata were played. "We'll see." She patted his hand and turned her head to the front, watching the cellist and the pianist play with rapt attention.

Everton did the same for a while, but his eyes soon wandered around the room. Lady Gertrude was sat beside Her Grace, with Miss Jessup to her right at the very front of the ballroom. The Cormicks and the

Spencers had taken a row to the middle of the room and were strung out in a long line. Poor Miss Knorr was right at the very end of that row, looking very alone as Henry and Caroline continued to follow the music on the pages in front of them. He gave her a supportive smile. She beamed back at him. She looked radiant tonight, and he couldn't help wondering if there was a reason for it and felt a pang of jealousy for whoever it might be for. Yet she did not seem to be glancing at anyone in particular. She was, as always, attentive to her charge, and warm with her friends.

Everton turned back to the musicians, but his mind would not settle on the music. He felt on edge. He wanted to ask Miss Knorr why she looked so particularly lovely tonight. He needed to know who it was she had dressed for tonight. He had never felt such a surge of jealousy in his life – not even when he had courted Katherine and feared that someone else might gain her hand before he did. He had no claim over Miss Knorr and had believed himself to be uninterested in a relationship with anyone – yet, here he was now, green with envy of he knew not who.

By the time the musicians had finished playing, Everton was almost apoplectic. He wanted to rush to Miss Knorr's side, to demand she give him answers. But instead, he forced himself to go straight outside to try and cool off and gain some perspective. Lady Gertrude saw him flee and followed him outside. "Are you quite alright?" she asked him, her eyes full of concern.

"I am quite well," he assured her. "It was just a little stuffy inside."

"I did not mean physically," she said drily. "I know you are as hale and hearty as anyone. You seem out of sorts."

"As always, you are too observant by half," he told her. "I think I was just nervous for Henry, but I think the introductions have gone very well, don't you?"

"I think you are only telling me half the truth, but I agree. The Spencers truly made every effort to look and act their very best, did they not. I am sure that Miss Knorr's influence has been a help there. She knows how to set an example, don't you think?"

Her words lit up the darkness in his brain. "Of course, you are quite right," he said to Lady Gertrude. "That is why Miss Knorr has made such an effort tonight."

Lady Gertrude grinned. "Ah, you noticed that did you?" she said. "And is that why you are so discombobulated?"

"I don't know what you mean," Everton protested.

"I think you do," she said enigmatically. "I shall leave you to your pondering. I do hope that you can regain your composure soon, or you'll miss any chance you might have to take her through to supper. I saw Captain Crawley looking her way a number of times through the performance."

He knew she was teasing him, but Everton growled. "You are a minx," he told her. "I should have your brother whip you for your impertinence."

"But he is not here, and would not do such a thing anyway," she said, poking out her tongue as she disappeared back inside.

Left alone, with no company other than his own thoughts, Everton pondered what had come over him. He had been so sure that he would never love anyone again after losing Katherine. It had hurt him too much to lose her and he could not bear the thought of having to go through such pain ever again. Yet Miss Knorr had crept into his heart, almost without his even noticing her do so. He loved to see her smile. He could hardly wait to hear her opinion on matters, of import and of no consequence. When something good happened, he longed to celebrate it with her – and if something bad occurred, he needed to talk it over with her.

He peered through the glass door before re-entering the ballroom. Lady Gertrude had been quite right. Captain Crawley was indeed hovering a little too close by Miss Knorr and seemed determined to stake his claim to her. Yet she seemed to have barely even noticed the man's presence. Everton couldn't help smiling at that. She was as much a force of nature, in her own way, as Lady Gertrude.

Taking a deep breath, Everton made his way back inside and rejoined his family. His father and Mr. Spencer seemed to have already decided upon a number of projects that they hoped to work together on – and were now discussing terms for the marriage. Mama and Mrs. Spencer were talking with the duchess, who was an old friend of his mother's. Henry and Caroline were wrapped up in one another, as they always were, and Miss Jessup and Miss Knorr were trying to ignore the attentions of Captain Crawley and his friend Elias Savage.

A little way away Lady Gertrude was flirting with Lord Stavely and Captain Wilkins, and obviously enjoying having the two of them try so hard to win her favor. To have such confidence, so young, was something truly to be envied, Everton thought as he watched her control the conversation and both men with an ease that few possessed. Wycliffe really need not have worried about his little sister in his absence. Lady Gertrude could more than take care of herself.

The gong announcing supper rang. Everton hurried forwards just as Captain Crowley offered Miss Knorr his arm to escort her into the dining room. "Dreadfully sorry, old chap," he said to the rather put out officer as he slipped between Crawley and Miss Knorr, "but I asked before the musicale commenced." Crawley frowned, but stepped back with a gracious bow.

"Thank you," Miss Knorr whispered as they began to move away from him. "He is such a dreadful bore."

"I shall take that as a compliment that I am not," Everton teased.

"Indeed, you should," Miss Knorr assured him, grinning back. "You are most certainly never dull."

"I am very glad to hear it," he said, feeling happier than he had in some time. He shook his head, almost imperceptibly, as he marveled at how this young woman had managed to break down his defenses, without ever realizing that she had done so. He did not doubt that she just thought him polite and well-mannered when he offered to dance with her, or escort her into supper. He needed to make her see that there was so much more to his gallantry than that, though he had no idea how – and little time to do so. If she truly meant what she had said about leaving London to return to Devon once Miss Spencer was wed, then he barely had a month in which to win her heart.

CHAPTER THIRTEEN

J*une 1820, London*

THE SPENCER HOUSEHOLD immediately erupted into a flurry of frenzied activity. The dressmaker was called first. She arrived with four assistants carrying reams and reams of the finest silks, satins, velvets and other fabrics so Caroline might choose her trousseau. Caroline cared little for such matters, other than her clothing feel soft against her skin, so Mrs. Spencer and Anne made most of the decisions as to what she might need. Once the choices required for every gown and undergarment had been made, the plans for her wedding gown were discussed in minute detail. Anne was utterly fatigued by it all – and she enjoyed being fitted for gowns and discussing fashion. She could only imagine how Caroline must be feeling, given the poor girl hated such things.

Then came the discussions about venues and flowers, whether to have a large Society event, or a smaller more intimate one. Naturally, Caroline and Henry both preferred the latter – but given the scandal before their betrothal it was decided that a large wedding to show everyone just how in love the young couple were would be best. Added to all of these concerns was the round of appearances that the couple were expected to make in the run-up to their nuptials. They found themselves wanted by every Society hostess and were inundated with invitations. It was never-ending, and everyone was soon weary and fractious.

The only benefit, if there was such a thing, in the mad frenzy of anticipation and arrangements, was that Anne got to see Everton Cormick almost every day. He was ever present. Anne presumed it was to smooth any issues that might arise with his easy to rile brother, but it made her days pass more easily, and in much better humor than might have otherwise occurred. Neither Henry Cormick nor Caroline was suited to the amount of attention they were now subject to. They would happily have spent their days in the country, alone, away from Society and all its expectations. Both had fraying tempers and struggled to behave as was expected without a large amount of intervention from Anne and Mr. Cormick.

Despite or perhaps because of all the hustle and bustle, the wedding was soon upon them, with a combination of excitement, frustration and sadness on Anne's part. She couldn't help thinking about what her own life would be like once Caroline and Henry were wed. No longer required as a companion, she would be packing her bags and returning to Devon and might never see Mr. Cormick, Lady Gertrude or any of the other friends she had made in Society in the past few years for a very long time – if ever – again. She tried not to think on that too often, as it made her sadder than she could have ever expected it to.

Of course, she was delighted for Caroline. Every day, despite the difficulties the pair faced in order to act as a happy couple was expected to, Caroline and Henry seemed to grow closer and closer together. Every spare moment they could muster, they would be found in the relative peace and quiet of the library, poring over books and then discussing them with fierce passion and commitment. It was quite something to watch.

"They truly were made for one another," Everton Cormick noted, coming up behind Anne as she leaned against the library door watching the pair as they escaped the party thrown in their honor by Lady Gertrude on this, the night before their nuptials. Both sat upon the sofa by the fire, their noses buried in books, their bodies so close they could be touching, yet there was no contact as that would be improper.

"I believe they were," Anne said, turning to face him for a moment. He looked tired, but handsome in his evening suit. She longed to be able to reach up and push back the stray hairs that had escaped the ribbon at his nape, to caress his cheek, but instead she kept her hands folded demurely before her.

"I am so glad you brought them together," he said, unexpectedly taking her hands in his. Anne found herself unable to focus on what he was saying to her, if he was saying anything at all. Her breath was suddenly coming very quickly. Anne was unsurprised to feel the same jolt of energy and fizzing pleasure as she had when their hands had brushed accidentally, all those weeks ago in the library. She did not want it to stop, it was such an invigorating sensation. Anne wondered if he had felt it, too, the surge had been so powerful, so strong. Time seemed to slow down and speed up all at the same time, leaving Anne feeling quite peculiar.

The moments ticked by. Mr. Cormick inclined his head towards her, his eyes looking into hers. Anne held her breath, wondering if he might press a kiss to her lips. He drew closer and closer. Anne's breath caught. She didn't dare to even move that much in case it shattered the moment. But, suddenly and without warning, he pulled away and stepped back from her. "I cannot thank you enough. You shall forever have my entire family's gratitude."

"It was nothing," Anne assured him, nervously fidgeting with her hair as the pair then stood in silence. It truly hadn't been hard to get them together, she had simply been testing a hunch that had turned out to be right. She turned back to look at Caroline and Henry. It was easier than looking at Mr. Cormick, especially now.

She wondered, for a moment, if she had perhaps seemed too eager for his kiss and that was why he had pulled away. No young woman in Society should act like a wanton. She was sure she had not been, but who was to judge what might be deemed too much? She had been too caught up in his beautiful blue eyes and had lost control of herself in that breathlessly exciting moment in a way she had never done before. Mr. Cormick made her feel things she knew that she shouldn't be feeling, but she couldn't seem to stop herself.

"Do you leave immediately after the ceremony?" he asked her a few moments later, his voice unusually tentative.

"No, I shall attend the dancing afterwards, and see Caroline and Henry off to the countryside after lunch the next day. Then, Lady Gertrude has offered me the use of her carriage to return to my home."

"I am surprised she did not offer you a position with her," Mr. Cormick said. "I was so sure she might. She is very fond of you, and I know she wished to make you her companion before you were employed by the Spencers."

Anne smiled sadly. "I will not displace dear Miss Jessup. She and Lady Gertrude suit one another well, and I must confess to be glad to return home to spend some time in peace and quiet after all this chaos." It was partly true. Anne had not seen her family in a very long time, and she longed to see them and to enjoy the peace and quiet of the cozy manor house she had grown up in. But she had grown fond of Caroline and Henry, Lady Gertrude, and Miss Jessup, and of course, the man who stood by her side. She feared she would miss him most of all.

"That is a shame," Mr. Cormick said, his voice full of regret. Anne turned to face him once more. He looked truly saddened by her departure. "You will be much missed by many here in London," he added in a clipped tone. And with that said, he had turned and walked away.

Anne was left standing alone in the hallway, unsure as to what had just passed between them. She didn't dare hope that Mr. Cormick felt anything more for her than just friendship – yet he had acted as if he might. She shook herself down. It mattered little what he might or might not feel. That he felt he could not speak of it, with her so close to leaving, meant that he never would. Anne knew that he would be expected to make a better match than her – the daughter of an impoverished baron, trying desperately to improve his position in life.

But she was not free to speculate further, as Mrs. Cormick came and chivied Caroline and Henry back to the party, insisting they dance and speak with their host, Lady Gertrude, even if they spoke with nobody else. Anne found herself being called upon by a number of young gentlemen to dance, but unusually Mr. Cormick had not claimed a one of them.

At the end of the evening, the Spencers and the Cormicks were the last to leave Lady Gertrude's party. As everyone made their goodbyes and thanked Lady Gertrude for hosting such a wonderful evening's entertainment, Henry and Caroline were, as always, reluctant to part, even though they would never need be parted again after tomorrow. Anne watched as the two families said their goodbyes and made little jokes about whether all would go well or not the next day. Surprisingly, they had grown close and found much in common. Everton clapped Henry on the back as the brothers climbed into Everton's phaeton, while Mr. and Mrs. Cormick took the more stately barouche behind.

Mr. Spencer offered his hand to his wife, who got

into their carriage with a little difficulty. The weather had been unseasonably damp and it had made her joints stiff and sore, though she did all she could to hide her discomfort whilst they were in company. Anne and Caroline got into the carriage behind them. Caroline held Anne's hand, unexpectedly, the entire way home and almost dragged Anne up to her bedchamber once they arrived.

"Do you think all will be well?" she asked anxiously, as she kicked off her dancing slippers. "I mean, after tomorrow. I know full well that tomorrow will be a nightmare." She sighed dramatically.

"Tomorrow will be wonderful," Anne said firmly. "You will enjoy it much more than you expect to. I know you don't truly enjoy large affairs, but it will be different."

"I know I cannot wait to see Henry's home in the country. We will stay there for three months, at least. He assured me of it."

"That is certainly the plan," Anne agreed.

"He has told me of their library, and how quiet it is in Hertfordshire. It shall be bliss."

"Do you not care to visit their hunting lodge in Scotland? I would imagine it is possibly even more secluded and remote," Anne teased.

"But it will not have a library," Caroline said. "How can it, if it is just a lodge?"

Anne shook her head. Caroline could be so very literal sometimes. "Get a good night's rest," she said as Caroline's lady's maid appeared to help the young woman get ready for bed.

"I doubt I shall sleep a wink," Caroline said as the maid helped her out of her dress and into a nightgown. "I am too excited. Will you not stay with me? Without you, I would not have made it this far. I need you." The maid put the dress away and fetched Caroline's hairbrush. Caroline took it and tapped it on the palm of her hand.

Anne was touched. It was the nicest thing she'd ever heard from her young mistress. "Of course, I will stay if you wish me to."

"I shall miss you," Caroline said as Anne sat down beside the young woman on the bed and began to unpin her hair. Caroline handed her the brush, and Anne began to ease it gently through Caroline's long, curled hair. Once it was soft and smooth, Anne plaited the silken blond tresses neatly ready for bed. Caroline sank back against the sheets. "I have never much liked being touched," she admitted as Anne put the brush back on the dresser. "Do you think it will be as terrible as Mama said, tomorrow night, with Henry?"

Not knowing what Mrs. Spencer had told her daughter about her wedding night, Anne did not know how to respond. Anyway, it wasn't as if she had any knowledge of such things herself. "I don't know," she said eventually. "I can only hope he will be gentle and loving with you."

"He will be, he is a gentle man, is he not?" Caroline looked at Anne anxiously. "He would not hurt me?"

"I am sure he would not," Anne said, and she was as sure of that as she could be of anything. Henry clearly cared very much for Caroline, in his own peculiarly cold way. Anne doubted he would do anything to hurt her. It wasn't in his nature. He was curious, clever and a little distracted – but he was never intentionally unkind, even though he could be as blunt and direct as Caroline herself could be. "I believe the two of you are going to be so very happy, you will not even notice that I am gone."

Caroline smiled, then laid down and closed her eyes. Anne laid down beside her and waited until the young woman's breathing slowed and steadied, when she got up, blew out the lamps and retired to her own chambers. She got ready for bed herself and lay down in her own bed. She closed her eyes and prayed that sleep would claim her quickly, but it seemed that it was not to be. She lay awake, tormented by everything that she would be saying goodbye to.

Her departure had arrived without her having much time to think on it. There had been so many other things to consider. Yet it was almost here now, and she would soon be saying her goodbyes – not just to Caroline and Mrs. Spencer, but to Lady Gertrude, Henry, Miss Jessup - and to Everton Cormick. She had been so sure he had intended to kiss her tonight. She had wanted him to kiss her tonight. It would have ruined her own reputation – but she would have let him kiss her tonight.

She did not know how it had happened, but her affections for him had grown so strong, especially since they had spent so much time together planning this unexpected wedding. He had shown such patience with his mercurial and oftentimes difficult brother. He was able to diffuse moments when it looked as though Henry might dig in his heels and refuse completely, winning him over – as Anne had done much the same with Caroline. And he had often managed to do so with a gentle humor and always with kindness.

She would miss him most of all, and she had not expected that when she had set out from Devon all those years ago, to become Mary Durand's companion. She had already accepted that she would not ever find the happiness of a good match. She could have settled for something less than that, and many people had told her she was a fool to write that off so young. But Anne had known that she could not have lived contentedly in a marriage that did not suit her, where there was no love.

And so, she had accepted that she would remain unwed. She had applied herself to her position and had found much enjoyment in the company of Mary and her dear father. Things had not been so easy, once Anne had come to work for the Spencers, but she had grown fond of them, for all their uncouth ways. They were fiercely loyal people, and Anne knew that they had grown fond of her in their own way, too. Yet it was not Mr. Durand, Caroline or anyone else she would miss the most. That honor would belong to Everton Cormick, who had won her heart without ever even trying to do so.

CHAPTER FOURTEEN

J*uly 1820, London*

THE DAY of his brother's wedding dawned brightly, with only the barest handful of clouds scudding through the blue skies. Everton washed and dressed quickly before heading to his brother's rooms, where he found Henry up – and unexpectedly, already attired in his fine new suit for the wedding, his hair neatly brushed and tied with a ribbon. "Oh," Everton said as he came to an abrupt halt in the doorway.

"You expected me to still be abed, did you not?" Henry said with a grin as he got up and moved towards his older brother. "Well, I am glad to have done something to surprise you, brother."

"You truly can't wait, can you?" Everton said with a grin.

"No, I cannot. I have never expected to think on marriage as the best situation that might be open to me. It always seemed to be a lot of fuss and nonsense, but I am looking forward to making Miss Spencer, Caroline, my bride."

"And we are all glad of it," Everton said, slapping Henry on the back affectionately.

"And what of you?" Henry said with a small frown. "Even I can see that you are fighting with yourself, torn between your memories and the future you deserve to have with Miss Knorr."

"My what...?" Everton spluttered. He had not confided his feelings for Miss Knorr to anyone. He had barely acknowledged them to himself. Yet, if Henry could speak of them with such confidence – and as he said, he was not the most observant of men – then Everton had not been as discrete about them as he had imagined.

"Come, brother. You are not truly surprised that everyone knows? You spend every moment you can in her company. I have not seen you smile, nor laugh, as often as you do with her, since long before dear Katherine passed away. We lost you, for such a long time. She has brought you back to us."

Everton had not thought on it that way. He had not realized how much of him had gone into the grave with his lost love. Henry clearly had. Presumably, so had his parents – and probably many of his friends. He wondered why nobody had ever spoken to him of it – then realized that he had not given anyone a chance to delve into anything of any import in many years now. He had kept all his encounters on a superficial level he would have despised in himself before. Until he had met Miss Knorr, who had somehow managed to dig deeper.

"Are you truly going to let her go?" Henry asked him, his face serious.

"What do you mean?"

"She leaves for her home tomorrow. She has told Caroline that she does not expect to ever visit London again."

"She definitely won't be taking another position next Season?" Everton asked, surprised at such a thing. He had known that Miss Knorr intended to return home after the wedding but had presumed that she would find a new position and would return in due course.

"As far as I know," Henry confirmed, "she has no intention of finding a new position. You don't have time, brother, if you had assumed that you might take things slowly and continue your non-courtship of her next Season." He raised an eyebrow and chuckled. Everton bristled.

He turned away, unable to think clearly. If what Henry said was true, then he did not have time on his side. This was a problem. Everton knew he had come a long way in the past weeks. He had begun to let Katherine's memory rest, and he was at peace with that now. He had learned to be himself again, to be more open, to let himself have real fun once more. Not the shallow pastimes that he had lost himself in to hide his misery from everyone around him, the drunken parties and the flirtations that meant little to him and even less to his paramours. But those amusements had never truly distracted him. He had always felt guilty and ashamed of his actions. He realized that since meeting Miss Knorr, he had not felt guilt or shame. She made him want to be the man he had been before. And he had been that man. He had been happy.

But he wasn't ready to fully commit Katherine to the past. She had been the love of his life. He could not deny that he had feelings for Miss Knorr – perhaps had even come to love her – but he did not feel for her the way he had for Katherine. Would it be fair to make a commitment to Miss Knorr, to ask for her hand, if he was unsure if he would ever be able to think upon her in that way? She did not deserve a lifetime of being anyone's second choice. And did he really deserve a second chance at love? It had not gone so well the first time around – what if he lost Miss Knorr, too? Would there be anything of him left to survive that? Did he dare to take the chance? Would it be fair to Miss Knorr if he did, and then could not be the man, the husband that a woman like her deserved?

Thankfully, he was saved from having to answer his own questions by the need to get Henry to the church. He rushed Henry into his phaeton and drove swiftly and skillfully along the London streets to the church. Henry didn't stop smiling, even as the guests began to arrive and insisted upon greeting him. He was unusually polite and welcoming. Everton was certain it wasn't the influence of his wife-to-be, as she could be as standoffish as he himself was. His mother had never been able to change Henry's behavior either, so Everton couldn't help wondering what had come over him. He was grateful of it, though.

But as Miss Spencer appeared at the end of the aisle, dressed in a simple white gown, her hair piled high upon her head, with seed pearls and flowers tucked in amongst her blonde curls, Everton couldn't help seeing his lost love and not his brother's bride. Miss Spencer resembled Katherine so very much, it was hard not to think that she had come back from the grave to marry him, after all this time. It almost came as a shock to Everton when her father placed her hand in Henry's and not his own.

And in that moment Everton knew he had the answer to the question that he had been trying to avoid for weeks now. He was not ready to love another. Katherine's hold over his heart was still too great, if he could forget and see Katherine in Caroline Spencer, if his imagination was still playing such tricks upon him, he could not in all good conscience offer himself to another – even if that someone was the sweet, kind and lovely Miss Knorr.

Shaking his head and trying to banish such thoughts, Everton stood at Henry's side throughout the ceremony. He handed his brother the ring when called upon and smiled reassuringly at both bride and groom as they began to falteringly make their vows to one another. He was still surprised and very touched by the affection this unusual pair held for one another. But his gaze continued to be pulled back to Miss Spencer, wishing he had been able to stand at the altar of this church with Katherine and to be making the vows that this young woman who looked so very like her was making to his brother.

The ceremony drew to a close and he made his way out of the church behind Henry and his bride, now another Mrs. Spencer, walking alongside Miss Knorr. Everton could barely bring himself to look at her, keeping his eyes fixed straight ahead on the ribbon tying his brother's hair. She, thankfully, did not seem to notice how rude he was being to her – though he did feel bad about it. He just did not trust himself to speak with her after what had just occurred. He would not make things any harder for her. It was for the best that she would be returning to her home, for them both.

The wedding breakfast was delicious, and the company excellent, but Everton longed for solitude. He was glad when they all rose from the tables and went outside for some fresh air while the servants prepared the room for the evening's dancing. Everton escaped from the crowd and found a quiet spot in the gardens, where he could sit and think. Tears came to his eyes as he wondered whether Katherine would have looked as lovely as Caroline did today, had he and his lost fiancée ever reached their wedding day. He had so longed to spend his life with her, and nothing in his life had been as sweet, as good, as happy since she had been gone.

He buried his head in his hands and let himself sob. He had not cried, had not allowed himself to feel the sea of emotions that Katherine's death had left him with. He had feared that they might overwhelm him and that he might never come out from under them. Yet today it was as if they had taken matters into their own hands. He could not have stopped himself from crying, from feeling the hurt and the anger, the frustrations that he had been so unable to help her.

There was so much he had longed to say to her. So

many things he should have told her every single day – including how much he loved her, and how perfect she was in every way to him. Now he could barely even recall her image unless he had a portrait to look at, or Miss Spencer, now Mrs. Cormick stood before him. He remembered her always smelling of citrus and flowers, though could not recall which ones any longer. He wondered what she would say to him if she could see him now and could no longer hear her voice. But he wanted to. Oh, how he wanted to.

Everton didn't know how much time had passed when he finally looked up out of his hands and pulled out a handkerchief to wipe his eyes and nose. He hadn't heard the sound of the bell calling everyone back inside, nor the end of the chattering as people went in. He had not heard the sound of the orchestra as they began to play, or the laughter and happiness that the dancing brought to the guests. But he could hear it now, a dull hum somewhere in the near distance.

He stood up and took a deep breath, exhaling forcefully. It was the day of his brother's wedding. It was not right that he was sat out here feeling sorry for himself, when he should be inside, happy for Henry and Caroline. They deserved every happiness and he vowed that he would keep his morose countenance hidden behind a bright smile and cheery nature for the rest of the evening. He made his way inside. His mother frowned at him. She had clearly noticed his absence, but she did not scold him. She probably knew precisely what had kept him away. She always did.

He cheered and clapped as Henry and Caroline

danced a rousing jig and tried not to watch Miss Knorr as she executed every step perfectly and with her usual enthusiasm, showing up her partner and those in the square with her. But nobody cared. Everyone seemed to be having a good time, even the usually reticent bride and groom.

From time to time through the remainder of the evening Miss Knorr glanced over at Everton. She'd smile, and he'd smile back, but he did not claim a dance on her card, and nor did he seek her out to talk with when she wasn't dancing. He knew that she probably thought she had done something wrong. He wished he could assure her that she had not. But to do so would have meant him having to admit to why he could not bring himself to be near her, why he had to let her go – so she could be happy. He would only ever make her miserable. He was still wedded to a ghost, and it seemed that he would never be free.

CHAPTER FIFTEEN

October 1820, *Tulilly, Devon*

DEVON WAS LOVELY. After the hustle and bustle of London, it was bliss to be somewhere quiet and calm. The fields around Tulilly had been full of crops when Anne had arrived, not yet ready for harvest, and animals grazing contentedly. Anne had been able to enjoy long walks and read as much as she liked without fear of being interrupted. Yet the autumn months had soon followed, and now the days were colder, and she was confined to her old home more often. She loved the old manor house, with its heavy beams and wonky floors. Everything about the place was solid and real, cozy and comfortable – unlike the dainty, elegant townhouses being built in the cities. But there were sad memories here, too – and they did not always bring comfort.

As the days grew wetter and she had less to do to

occupy herself, Anne couldn't stop thinking about how distant Mr. Cormick had been in her final few days in the city. Perhaps she had done something to upset him? Perhaps he had thought her too wanton in that moment in the library? It had made enjoying the wedding celebrations so much harder than they should have been. Caroline and Henry had been so happy. They had shared an unexpectedly emotional farewell, and Caroline had made Anne promise to write often.

She was trying to do just that, as she gazed out of the window over the lawn of her father's manor house. But Anne had little to tell her. Nothing much happened in this part of the county, and if it did, Caroline would not know any of the people Anne might mention – nor much care for them. So, Anne wrote about a new book she had read instead. She would send a copy of it with her letter so that Caroline could read it to. Perhaps she might enjoy it and they could talk about it in their correspondence.

"Anne, would you assist me?" Papa asked, coming into the sunny parlor. His round face was pale, his brow furrowed. He scratched at his balding pate distractedly as he handed her a ledger and pointed to a line written in tiny script. "My eyesight is not what it once was, and my bailiff insists upon fitting everything into one line."

Anne smiled and took the ledger. She held it up to her face so she could take a closer look at the inky dots. "Three palomino ponies, four bay mares and a chestnut stallion," she said, squinting a little at it herself. "When did you buy new horses? I did not see them in the paddock, or the stables."

Her father exhaled forcefully. "I had so hoped that I

was wrong," he said sadly. "I did not buy new horses. We don't have the stabling, nor the need. I can barely afford to keep my stallion and the carriage horses, much less purchase new ones. I fear that there may be many similar entries." He sank down onto the sofa beside Anne. She reached out and took his hand in hers. He looked as thought he carried the weight of the world upon his shoulders. She wished there was something she could do to ease his burden.

"How could this have happened?" she asked. "I thought that your bailiff was one of the best in the county?"

"The man was recommended to me, had a character from Lord Wilcox. I took him on trust. I should not have done but, whilst your mother was unwell the other year, I did not pay the attention to our affairs that they required. It has taken me too long to get back on top of them, too. I only have myself to blame."

Anne knew that trying to reassure him otherwise would be futile. Her father was generally very astute. He would never have permitted such a thing to happen had he been in his right mind, but he had been so fearful of losing Mama when she had been ill and had never really recovered his composure since. Her illness had brought back too many memories of James, her brother's passing when he was just a boy. Everyone had feared that they would lose Mama too. Papa had aged ten years overnight when the doctor had told them that James had passed. He had aged an additional five when the doctor had told them he feared for Mama's survival and he seemed to age a year for every day that it took for her fever to break, every minute spent by her side willing her to recover.

"Would you like me to go through them," she suggested, wanting to be of use in whatever way she could, "to see if there are any further entries where large sums seem to have been paid out with nothing to show for it?"

Her father sighed gratefully. "My darling girl, I cannot tell you how much that would help me."

Anne smiled at him, squeezed his hand and the pair stood up and took the ledger over to the table by the window. She pulled out paper and pen and began to go through the pages and pages of entries since her mother was ill with influenza a few years previously. Thankfully, Mama had made a full recovery. Anne could only hope that her father's interests would recover as swiftly, and as completely. Papa paced around her nervously, like a caged big cat. By teatime, she had found a further twenty suspicious entries, and still had a further quarter's accounts to analyze. Papa had truly been taken for a fool and had lost almost a thousand pounds during each of the years concerned.

"It is so much worse than I could have imagined," her father kept saying each time they discovered a new entry that did not tally with an actual purchase, peering over her shoulder as if looking again might make it somehow different. "How could I not have seen this, happening under my very nose?"

There was little Anne could say to reassure him, and she knew that it would be almost impossible to get the money back – even though the man was currently unaware that they knew of his schemes. He would, of course be turned out without a character, and Anne was sure that her father would report him to the magistrate – but even if he was put in jail, that did not help to solve the family's financial concerns.

The housemaid appeared just as Anne set down her pen. "Yes, Heather, what is it?" Anne asked the young woman.

"A letter for Sir John," Heather said, handing over a letter to Anne's father. "From Lord William Cott, himself."

"Is there, indeed?" Anne mused. "He promised once that he would visit you, Papa and assist in any business matters if he was able to. So much has happened since then, that it had completely slipped my mind. I cannot help but think that if that is his intent, it could not have come at a more opportune moment."

"And also, a letter for you ma'am," she said, hurrying forward with the cream-colored parchment, sealed with red wax she held in her hand. "From your Lady Mary."

"Oh, how wonderful. I have not heard from Lady Mary in so long," Anne said happily, forgetting her father's troubles for just a moment. She opened it hastily and read it quickly. "Oh, Papa, Heather, it is wonderful news. They wish me to go and stay with them, and to act as godmother to their second child."

The girl smiled. "Aw, that's nice, Miss," she said. "Quite an honor." Her father merely nodded and continued reading his own missive.

"It is indeed, when you think of the company they keep," Anne said clasping the letter to her breast. A trip to Alnerton would be just what she needed to improve her increasingly melancholy mood. But how could she leave when her father needed her so badly? He had too much to contend with alone.

The maid grinned and then disappeared as Anne waited for her father to read his letter and tell her its contents. His facial expressions ranged through smiles and frowns, pensive and considerate to surprised and concerned. "Papa, what does Lord William say?" she prompted him, when he still hadn't spoken after almost ten minutes.

"He is to drive here to collect you himself," Papa said, rifling through the pages and going back to the start of the letter. "After you were unable to attend their first' child's baptism, they have no intention of permitting you to miss this one."

"That is kind of him, but I will write to him and tell him it is not necessary. I cannot leave you now."

"Don't be silly, of course you must go. I would not let you miss such a thing. What kind of father ever would?"

Anne gave him a sad smile. "And what kind of a daughter would it make me if I did not stay here to help you?"

"Tush," her father said dismissively. "You will pack your things, because looking at the date your Lord William sent this, it is too late anyway. He will already be on the road. And he also wishes to speak with me. There is a matter he needs assistance with and thinks I may be the man to help him."

The wait for Lord William's arrival felt interminably long, even though it was barely a week from receiving his letters until his eventual appearance. Anne greeted his carriage outside the house. Lord William was half leaning out of the carriage window as it rolled up the driveway and beamed as he saw Anne stood waiting. He waved enthusiastically, then bounded out of the carriage, almost before the carriage had come to a complete stop.

She bobbed a curtsey. He raised her up, clasping her hands and kissing her cheeks affectionately. "It is good to see you looking so well," he told her.

"And how is dear Lady Mary?"

"She is as besotted with baby Kingsley, as she was with young Nathaniel," Lord William assured her as she escorted him inside. "As are we all."

"And Lady Charlotte? Captain William? And their little one? They are all well?"

"They are, as are Mr. and Mrs. Watts," Lord William assured her.

"I am so glad."

"I know Mary can hardly wait to see you. She wanted me to bring the phaeton, so you would get back to Alnerton more quickly," he joked.

"I am glad you did not. That ride you took us on, scared me half to death," Anne laughed, remembering the time Lord William had driven her and Lady Mary to the village. It had been a hair-raising experience - one she had no desire to replicate.

"You did go terribly green," he said with a grin as Papa emerged from his study, forcing a smile.

"Lord Cott, I am honored beyond measure," Papa said, bowing politely. William stretched out a hand.

"I am grateful for your hospitality, Sir John Knorr,"

Lord William said taking it. The two men shook hands, firmly, each taking the other's measure. "And that you will permit us the pleasure of Anne's company once more. She has been much missed by us all."

"You do me great honor, my lord," Anne said humbly.

"Pish, 'tis the other way around, I can assure you. Now, my time here is, understandably, limited, so I do hope you will not mind if we talk business immediately, Sir John?" Anne nodded encouragingly at her father, who with a wave of his hand gestured that the two men should retire to his study.

A few hours later, Anne dressed quickly for supper and made her way downstairs at half past seven. Her father and Lord William were already in the parlor, enjoying a glass of sherry. Both were smiling and seemed completely at ease in one another's company. Anne looked from one man to the other. "So?" she asked expectantly.

"I think we should wait for your Mama," Papa said. He was obviously very content with the outcome. The ridges in his brow seemed to have unrumpled themselves and his worried frown had been banished from view. Anne was relieved, but impatiently intrigued. Thankfully, her mother appeared at that very moment.

"Mama, I would like to introduce you to Lord William Pierce," Anne said formally, "Earl of Cott."

Mama curtseyed gracefully and held out her hand. Lord William kissed it gallantly as he bowed down over it. "It is a pleasure, and I am so glad that your health seems so greatly improved now as well."

"I must confess, so am I," Mama said with a smile.

"Now, did I hear that there is news that you wish to tell us all?"

"You did," Papa said, puffing up his chest proudly. In his bright red waistcoat, he rather resembled a robin red breast. "Lord Cott and his father, the duke, have invested in an enterprise no more than ten miles from the village. They wish to hire a man to oversee it, and I am flattered that they immediately thought of me."

"What type of enterprise, Papa?" Anne asked as her father handed her and her mother a glass of sherry, too.

"It's a mine, Anne," Lord William said. "A tin mine, and there is also a dock and a shipbuilding yard. It has been badly run for a time, but I think with the right man at the helm it could be quite profitable for us all."

Anne was flattered that Lord William and his father had considered hers, but she worried that Papa had little experience with such matters, and that running such a complex enterprise might be beyond him – especially given what they had spent the afternoon unravelling together just a week ago. She forced a smile, but her parents and Lord William obviously all knew her too well. "You do not approve, Anne?" Lord William asked.

"It is not my place," she said, determined not to embarrass her father in front of Lord William.

"You mean the issues in the ledgers," Papa said softly, giving her a warm smile. "Don't worry, I have confessed all to Lord William. I would not wish him to enter into business with a man lying to him from the start. I know all too well how that feels." His tone was thick with emotion.

"I think we can all be sure that the concerns your

father has faced in recent years would be more than enough to distract any man," Lord William said. "I know a little of the concern around the possibility of losing the one you love to illness myself. I think we can safely say though, that your father is unlikely to ever get caught out by such a thing again. Experience, especially the unpleasant ones, seem to act as the finest teachers."

"I would never trust matters of such import to another, that is for certain," Papa insisted.

"You need not convince me, Papa," Anne assured him. "I know full well you will not. But I did not wish for Lord William or his father to be unaware."

Lord William nodded appreciatively. "And, dear Anne, you need not fear that I am only involving your father because of the promise I made to you. My father and I have been racking our brains for weeks to think of who might be best. My father's solicitor, John Watts, has been drawing up lists and lists of candidates and looking into them. Your father came up time and time again, recommended by no less than thirty companies who have dealt with him over the years. He is a local man, understands the local ways, and is honorable to a fault – or so we have been told by everyone who has ever met him or done business with him."

CHAPTER SIXTEEN

O *ctober 1820, Hertfordshire*

"I SHAN'T GO," Everton said setting down the letter that had just arrived from his old friend, William Pierce. "I am exhausted and can think of nothing worse than being surrounded by all those screaming babies that Charlotte and William seem to insist upon having all the time."

Henry looked up from his book, and chuckled. "You say that, as if you wish to mean it," he said. "But I don't believe you actually do."

Everton sighed. "You are right, I do not mean it. I am rather fond of their children. In the main, they seem to be very well-behaved and actually rather clever."

"So, why do you really not wish to attend?"

Everton didn't think he could possibly admit that he was afraid that Miss Knorr might have been invited. He knew how close her friendship with Lady Mary was, and how much Miss Knorr had hated not being able to attend William and Mary's first child's christening. If she was not bound to a household now, and he hadn't heard anything to suggest that she had taken on a new charge, then she would be free to attend – and he did not wish to make anything uncomfortable for her – or his old friends.

"It is Miss Knorr, isn't it? You keep avoiding everything because you fear you might see her there. I think it is perfectly clear, from her letters to Caroline, that she is safely ensconced in the country, miles away from here. I think you have little to fear – and William would be most put out if you miss it. He has asked you to stand as godfather. It is not as if you would be any old guest."

Everton hated it when Henry was right – especially about matters such as this. If even he thought that Everton should attend, then he really ought to. Henry was so adept at discovering excuses not to attend events he did not wish to. If he could not think of a reason why Everton should not go, then there was none.

"Then I had best get myself packed and on the road," he said with regret. Henry was probably right. Miss Knorr would be most unlikely to be in attendance. And even if she was, it wasn't as if they had parted on bad terms – just somewhat silent ones on his behalf. He had felt bad about it ever since. He should have spoken to her. It wasn't her fault that her charge was the very image of his lost love. Months of living with Caroline had assured him most completely that she was nothing like his Katherine, as he had always known - and he had come to be a little more settled in his emotions once more.

He could not deny that there were still moments when he missed Katherine. But, as it had been before his brother's nuptials, he had accepted that would always be the way of things – and that it was time to let her rest in peace while he did his best to honor her memory. He knew that remaining unmarried and alone was not the way to do that. She would have hated to think of him pining endlessly for her.

"When will you admit to yourself that you love her, brother?" Henry said suddenly, interrupting Everton from his thoughts. "You cannot keep running from that."

"I do not," Everton protested, but then paused. Again, if even Henry had noticed such a thing, it had probably been obvious to everyone else for months. He had believed that he had been circumspect, in order to protect her reputation. And he had distanced himself from her as soon as his feelings had grown too complicated – or at least he had tried to. Perhaps it had already been too late by then.

He missed her, every single day. The end of the Season had been dreadfully dull without her there to talk with and dance with. Even the king's coronation had seemed dull and lifeless – despite Prinny's determination to make it a grand spectacle. Miss Knorr had become the barometer by which he measured his own enjoyment of an event – and without her there, he enjoyed almost nothing.

With an exasperated sigh, he stomped out of the library and up to his chambers. His valet, Jenkins, was awaiting him. "How do you always know when I have need of you?" Everton asked him.

"It is my job to know," Jenkins said with an unexpected grin. "Servants always know everything before their masters, and so things become easy to anticipate."

"I know that to be true," Everton said with a wry smile. "Things could be very different if some servants stood up and told all they know."

"Not here, though, sir," Jenkins said. "Your family have remarkably few secrets."

Everton chuckled. "Oh, the secrets are there," he said, "just ask Kingsley."

Jenkins laughed. "I doubt anyone knows his secrets. Never known a man like him." He paused. "I've taken the liberty of calling for a couple of the maids to assist with your packing, sir. I hope you don't mind."

"Not at all," Everton said. "I will need warm clothes, for indoors and outdoors. There are some wonderful places to ride near Alnerton in the autumn. I have been invited to stay for two weeks, but father will need me back before then, so only need enough for one week. And, pack the royal blue velvet jacket for the baptism itself. I hope to leave at first light tomorrow. Thank you, Jenkins."

"My pleasure, sir." The young man gave a respectful nod, then began to pull out shirts and breeches, undergarments, waistcoats and jackets.

Everton left him to it. His father and mother were in London. He wondered if they too were packing in order to attend the baptism. He wouldn't be surprised if they had been invited as well. Through his contacts with the Duke of Compton, his father had been doing business with William's father, the Duke of Mormont, recently.

Given his own long-standing friendship and this strong connection, it would be quite rude if they had not been issued an invitation. He sincerely hoped that they would be there. He had not seen them for some months. When he was in Hertfordshire it was usually because his father was in London, and vice-versa – so that there was always someone present to oversee the family's interests in either location.

He ate a light supper that night and had an early night. He would have to set off at just after dawn in order to reach Alnerton before nightfall. He had done it in less, from time to time at break-neck speeds, but he was no neck-or-nothing rider and preferred to take his time when he could. He would stop at the Old Nag's Head for lunch on the way, where he would be able to enjoy a fine claret with an excellent steak and ale pie.

He slept surprisingly well and awoke with the dawn. His journey passed smoothly, and soon his carriage pulled onto the long driveway to Caldor House. He had not visited William in some time and was impressed by the changes made to the formal gardens in particular. They seemed to be full of colorful blooms now. Everton was sure that was down to Lady Mary, who adored flowers – especially roses. Cott was there to greet him with an affectionate slap on the back. "Good to see you, Cormick," he said proudly as he showed Everton inside. "Glad you could make it."

"I was honored to be invited. Are you truly sure you wish me to be your child's godparent? I'm not exactly cut out for it."

"No need to fear, the boy will have two other excellent godparents with much more esteemed characters than your own," Lord William teased. The men laughed together heartily.

Lady Mary emerged from one of the rooms off the grand hallway. "William, do try and keep it down. Both boys are in bed, and I know that myself and their nanny would like it to remain that way." She turned to Everton. "Welcome, Mr. Cormick. It is wonderful to see you again. We are so glad you could come. William will take you up to your rooms. I've had to put you in the green suite, as your usual rooms are already taken. I hope you don't mind."

"Lady Mary, you may set me to sleep in the stables if you need," Everton said gallantly, kissing the air above the back of his hostess' hand.

"I doubt that will be necessary," William said with a grin as he led Everton up the stairs. "The house is more than adequate to put up the guests we have. Sadly, your father could not get away from his work, but your Mama arrived earlier today. She is in the rooms next to yours. Claveston and Sophie are here, back from their trip in Europe, with Gertrude as well. So, you should find someone to amuse you, old chap."

"And I assume that your sister and James will be here from time to time?" Everton checked as they started to head down a narrow corridor on the second floor.

"Of course, try keeping Charlotte and Mary apart," William said, his contentment showing in every word and his entire face beaming with happiness. "She is determined that the children will all grow up as close friends and not just cousins."

"As it should be," Everton agreed.

William pushed open a door at the end of the corridor. Everton could immediately see why it was called the green room. Brocade drapes in lime green and silver adorned the windows, with matching ones on the ornately carved four-poster bed, which was covered with a matching counterpane. The walls were decorated in a dark green colored silk, with embroidered *fleur de lys* all over. His trunk already sat at the end of the bed, waiting for him. "I like it," he said sincerely. William chuckled again.

"I hate it," he admitted. "But each to their own. I'll leave you to freshen up. There's hot water on the washstand. Come down when you are ready. Dinner won't be served until you do."

William closed the door behind him, leaving Everton alone. He took off his jacket, pulled off his shirt and stared at himself in the mirror over the washstand. He could use a shave but there was not time if dinner was waiting for him. He poured water from ewer into the bowl and splashed some all over his face, neck and torso, before taking the soap and a cloth and washing himself more thoroughly. He dried himself carefully and rummaged in the trunk for a clean shirt and breeches.

Barely ten minutes later he was dressed, and on his way back down the stairs, his blonde floppy hair tied back as best he could ever manage. He was almost at the bottom of the first staircase when Miss Knorr emerged from one of the first-floor corridors. He paused, biting at his lip. "Good evening," he said as she looked up and saw him, her pretty mouth forming a perfect circle as she saw him there.

"I'm sorry, I didn't know you were expected," she said, awkwardly.

"Nor I you," he said. "But I am glad to see you, Miss Knorr. I must apologize for my dreadful behavior at Henry's wedding, and the lunch the following day."

"There is no need. We were both busy, there were so many people clamoring for everyone's attention. It was a wonderful day. I was so pleased for dear Henry and Caroline. How are they both? I am never entirely sure from Caroline's letters; she tends to talk only of things they have been studying."

Everton laughed. "They do not think such trivial things as how they are matter," he said. "But they are both well, and most content with one another. Henry is to return to Oxford. He has a position as a tutor to start and will be able to undertake the research he so loves and get paid to do it. Caroline and I rather insisted he tell my father that was what he wanted. Once she took that part, he seemed bolstered enough to do so."

"I am so glad," she said. "Though I can only presume that makes more work for you and your father?"

"It does, but it is worth it to see Henry so content. Father and I thrive on having much to occupy us." He was surprised at how quickly they had slipped back into their usual way of being with one another. He had missed this so much and hadn't known just how much until being here with Miss Knorr once more.

The clock in the hallway struck the quarter hour, intruding upon the unexpectedly intimate moment. "We should go down," Miss Knorr said a little nervously. "I hate to be late."

"I believe dinner is on hold until I make my appearance," Everton assured her. "So, you will not be considered late unless you arrive after me." He offered her his arm, and they made their way down the stairs.

CHAPTER SEVENTEEN

Anne could hardly believe she was walking down such a grand staircase on the arm of a gentleman like Everton Cormick. Though she was the daughter of a baron, the Society her family had moved in, back in Tulilly, had not been anything like the circles that Mr. Cormick moved in, and that she had been exposed to as a lady's companion in recent years. And now, here she was, a guest in her own right, on the arm of a man whose family were friends with royalty.

She had been to Caldor House before, of course, as Mary's companion, but as such she had not been a real part of the company. And in London with both Mary and Caroline she had attended some of the finest homes, the most rarified events and seen *the Ton* as few of her position would ever get to see them. She had not been there to be noticed, though. Nobody had escorted her anywhere. Her presence had been tolerated because of her role as a companion – not because she was wanted anywhere.

Yet from the first, this man had been different. He had always done what he could to make her feel welcome, to dance with her, to take her into supper, to talk with her and be her friend. She wasn't sure how, but she had forgotten how handsome he was, with his sandy blonde hair, and those spectacular blue eyes that looked only at you when he talked, so you felt like the only thing in the world that mattered. How could she have forgotten such things? Her feelings for him, feelings that she had believed she had put aside, flooded back, overwhelming her with their intensity.

As ever, just the feeling of his solid, warm body so close to her own, her hand resting lightly upon his arm filled her with anticipation and anxiety. Her stomach was full of butterflies and her mouth dry as she tried desperately not to give herself and her inappropriate feelings for him away. He could not ever look to a woman such as her. His family would have set their sights much higher for their first son.

Dear Henry might have been permitted to marry a merchant's daughter, an industrialist's daughter – but Anne had no doubt that Mr. and Mrs. Cormick would wish for Everton to be matched with someone with a title, or at least a fortune. She would have neither. Her father's baronetcy would pass to her cousin, entailed as it was upon the first male of the bloodline. And so, when Papa died, she and Mama would be retired to the tiny dower house at the end of the drive, whilst cousin William moved into the manor house – or most likely rented it out as his own estates were far grander than those he would inherit from Papa.

But such matters were not even worth thinking on. Anne banished them from her mind. She determined to enjoy her time here in Alnerton, to bask in the friendship of this kindly young man as much as she might, before she returned to her home and her quiet life in the country. The memories would be all she had to keep her warm, so she might as well make those memories as special as she could.

She smiled up at him, and he smiled back. He tucked his spare hand over hers as it lay on his arm and gave her hand a squeeze. "It is such a pleasure to see you once more," he said softly. "I feared that I might never do so again, and I was so ashamed of how I treated you in those final days."

"I am sure you had your reasons," she said, though she could not think what they might have been. She did not wish to dwell on the past though. She had this one week with Mary and Lord William, with Mr. Cormick and the other guests present here for the celebrations. She intended to make it as special as she could.

"I did, and I do hope I will be able to sit with you, somewhere quiet, whilst we are here this week, to tell you of them."

"There is no need," Anne said gently. But there was. She needed to know.

"There is every need," he said sincerely. "I owe you an explanation, and so much more."

His words were cryptic, and intrigued Anne, but as they reached the vast hallway on the ground floor and he led her towards the library where the other guests were waiting for them Anne expected him to leave her side so he might greet everyone else present, yet he did not. He kept her close, and they greeted everyone together, as if they were an established couple. It was disconcerting and delightful all at once.

The gathered company here at Caldor House was select, and though many of those present held titles, that was not in any way an essential part of the criteria used to assemble the guest list. Lord William and Mary had simply invited the people they loved the most. Anne had been very touched to be amongst them. But she hadn't expected Mr. Cormick to be here. She did not know why it hadn't occurred to her, after all he and Lord William had been friends for a very long time.

Yet, here he was, acting as he had through most of the last Season, smiling and teasing, a twinkle in his eye. True, he had apologized for his peculiar behavior at his brother's wedding, and insisted that he intended to explain to her why he had been so cold, so distant with her – but she did not know now, and that nagged at her. She hated that she might have done anything or said something that might have offended him. Yet now he was talking to her as he always had, as if she had imagined all of that awkwardness.

She couldn't help it. She still loved him. She had tried to convince herself that it had been just a passing attraction, that she had simply been flattered by his atten-tion and kindness. But with him here, beside her, her arm tucked through his, she could not deny the impact he had upon her heart. Anne felt ill at ease, yet where she belonged, her belly full of butterflies, yet she felt happier than she had done in months. She almost despised herself for being such a silly girl. Her crush would never – could never - be reciprocated.

As etiquette demanded, he had greeted his hosts first. Lord William and Lady Mary were standing by the window talking with Lady Charlotte and Captain James, Lord Wycliffe and Lady Sophie. Mr. Cormick led Anne to them, and they made polite small talk with the group of old friends and their new wives as a servant brought them both a glass of sherry. Mr. Cormick did all he could to ensure that Anne was fully included in the conversation, inviting her in with pertinent little questions and comments. As always, his manners were impeccable - and his charm only made Anne care for him more deeply.

"Your mother is here, old man," Lord William reminded Mr. Cormick, pointing to where Mrs. Cormick was seated on a chair by the fireplace, talking with Mrs. Watts. Mr. Cormick grinned. "Then I'd best say hello," he said a little sheepishly. He had still not let go of Anne's arm and she had not dared to pull away, and so as he went to greet his mother, Anne went with him.

"I wondered when you would notice me," Mrs. Cormick said as her son finally let Anne's hand go and bent down to hug her and kiss his mother's cheek. She patted his fondly and beamed at him. As he did so, something fell out of his pocket. Anne reached for it, picking it up just before Mr. Cormick himself could bend down to retrieve it. His eyes were full of something that almost resembled fear. But what could he possibly be carrying that might make him so afraid? Anne glanced at the object. It was a miniature portrait, framed in gold, of a young woman who bore more than a passing resemblance to Caroline. Yet somehow Anne knew it was not Caroline in the picture. She took a deep breath and looked at him, wondering if this might be part of the explanation he had intended to give to her later.

He now looked awkward, like a boy caught climbing up to the highest shelf in the kitchens to steal a biscuit from the jar. "Thank you," he said stiffly, holding out his hand for the miniature. She handed it back to him, her eyes wide.

"That is why you were often so…" she tailed off. It wasn't the right place to discuss the matter. But he nodded as if he knew exactly what she had been about to say.

The gong for dinner sounded, and everyone began to move into the dining room. Anne felt totally confused. Nobody else seemed to have noticed a thing, and for that she was glad. Mr. Cormick seemed quite ill at ease as it was, the last thing he needed was for anyone to make a big thing of what had been a very private and very intimate moment, only the two of them – and possibly his mother – had shared. Mr. Cormick offered his mother his arm this time, as was right, leaving Anne to enter the dining room alone. She had never felt so lonely, especially given she was amongst friends, as she followed them all into the wood-paneled dining room.

The vast oak table had been set with the finest silver table settings, with the most gorgeous floral display running down the center that Anne had ever seen. Yet it brought her no joy. She took her seat, next to Captain Watts and Mr. Durand, Lady Mary's father. Mr. Cormick was seated by Lady Sophie and Mary on the opposite side of the table. He smiled at her a little ruefully, as if he wished he had been seated more closely to her so they might continue to talk – but Anne could not be sure if that was what he meant at all. After what had just happened, she did not know what to make of anything.

Why did he have a miniature in his pocket of a woman that could have been Caroline's twin? Why did he seem so ashamed of it? Or was it that he was afraid of her reaction? And if that was the case, why should he be so concerned about that? They had no understanding. There was nothing more than friendship between them, at least on his part. Thoughts raced through her mind, blurring out the conversations occurring all around her, trapping her in an ever more maddening cycle of anxious fretting as to what any of it meant. It ruined what should have been a joyous evening for her.

The meal was delicious, but Anne could hardly bring herself to eat more than a few mouthfuls. She forced herself to talk politely with the two gentlemen on each side of her, though she barely heard a word of their replies. She drank only a few sips of the claret in her glass, and tapped at it nervously with her fingertips each time she did, pausing unintentionally as her concerns crowded out her mind. She was not sure why she should feel so discombobulated. After all, she and Mr. Cormick had spent many months eating at the same table, dancing together and conversing often – and in much more intimate settings than this. Yet here, surrounded by their friends, with so much unspoken between them, Anne felt totally exposed and ill at ease with him. She feared she might give herself away, that she might ruin everything.

The meal seemed to go on forever. Course after course of delicious food appeared just as Anne thought they must be nearing its end. She tapped her feet under the table, her leg twitched nervously when she did not. She tried to smile, to pay attention to what was happening around her, and was actually surprised when the ladies all started to get up from the table to leave the men to their cigars and port. She had not even noticed that the last course had been sweeter than the others, as she had barely tasted anything properly all night.

She followed the ladies into one of the many parlors here at Caldor. Lady Sophie took a seat at the pianoforte and began to play, as Lady Charlotte and Lady Mary served everyone with ratafia and sweet biscuits. Mary paused as she handed Anne her glass and the little plate with the delicate treats set upon it. "Are you quite well, my dear?" she asked.

"I think I have a bit of a headache," Anne admitted. It was true enough. All those thoughts whirling through her brain were making it hurt. "Would you mind if I just took a little walk in the grounds?"

"Not at all. Would you like some company?" her friend asked.

"No, you should remain with your guests," Anne reminded her, setting down the glass and plate that Mary had just given to her. "I shall not be long."

Mary gave her hand a squeeze and a supportive smile. "Be as long as you wish," she said gently. "The gardens are very soothing, I always find."

CHAPTER EIGHTEEN

Everton could hardly wait to get away from the crowd of people surrounding him. He had intended to explain everything to Anne, it was why he'd brought the miniature with him – so she might understand why he had been so strange on Henry and Caroline's wedding day. And now, she had seen the portrait – but did not have any understanding of its significance. He could have kicked himself for being so careless. He should have left it in his room, until he was able to find a quiet moment to speak with her. If only he hadn't met her on the stairs like that. It had reminded him of just how much she meant to him. How much he longed for there to be no secrets between them – and then he had unwittingly added more.

He glanced around the room. The older men present were huddled at one end of the table, no doubt talking business. His friends, at the other end were all joking and laughing with one another. None of them seemed to notice he wasn't joining in. Perhaps they would not notice if he got up from his place and went outside for a walk to clear his head. He needed to think what to do. What should he say, to explain it all to Miss Knorr? She had looked so disappointed in him, so shocked that he would carry with him what she must have assumed was a portrait of his sister-in-law.

Quietly, he stood up and made his way out through the French doors onto the wide stone terrace. He moved towards the balustrade, leaned on it and looked out over the moonlit gardens. He sighed heavily as he pulled out the miniature of Katherine and stared at her lovely face. He truly had made such a mess of absolutely everything. He did not know how he would ever be able to put any of it right. "This is why you should never have left me, my darling," he whispered. "I am a mess without you to tell me what to do all the time."

He looked up and was surprised to see a lone figure walking between the flower beds of the formal garden. He knew it was Miss Knorr. She had such a definite, yet graceful manner of moving and the tilt of her head was quite peculiar to her. "Is this a sign?" he asked the portrait. "Are you telling me to just get on with it, to tell her everything and see where it takes me?"

He tucked the miniature back into his pocket and slowly made his way down the ornamental stone steps into the gardens. His long strides meant he soon caught up to Miss Knorr. He cleared his throat as he drew close, so she wouldn't be shocked by his sudden appearance. "It seems I have so much more to apologize to you for," he said with wry humor.

She turned slowly, her face lit up by the brightness of

the full moon. She looked almost ethereal she was so lovely. "You need not explain anything," she said. "We have never been more than friends."

"Oh, I think we both know that is most certainly not true," Everton said giving her a disbelieving look.

"I am," she paused, or should I say "was" a lady's companion only. It is not my place to assume that there is anything more than an acquaintanceship between myself and those within the circle of my employers." Her voice sounded strange, almost monotone as she said the words that any servant should say.

"You were much more than Caroline's companion to me. I do so hope you know that," he assured her fervently. "I have counted you as a very dear friend for quite some time."

Her expression was so full of hope, it made Everton's heart almost break for her as he realized the harm that he must have done to her for her to think that he did not care for her. But she composed herself once more. "Mr. Cormick, how should I know that? We have never spoken of such matters."

"I know, and I am sorry for that," he admitted. "I should have been much more clear about my feelings for you."

She shook her head. "There was no need. I should have never assumed anything more than my place with Caroline."

"Nonsense," Everton said, feeling unexpectedly angry. Why was she making all of this so easy on him? He had been unkind, rude and even untruthful to her – and she was assuming any fault was her own for thinking that a servant could ever have a friendship with him.

He inhaled deeply. "I think we should start from the beginning," he said trying to keep calm. "Miss Knorr, I am sorry – more sorry than you will ever know – for the manner in which I treated you on your final days in London. It was unforgiveable – whatever your position in Society. I was rude and unkind. You did not deserve me to be either."

"It was very unlike you," Miss Knorr said softly. "I couldn't help thinking that you blamed me for being too forward, for that moment in the library."

"Being too forward?" Everton couldn't stop himself from exploding. "You were not forward, you have never behaved inappropriately in all the time I have known you. But I wanted to."

"You did?" she asked, wide-eyed with surprise.

"Did you not feel it, even the first time we danced at Wycliffe's wedding? You were, are perfect, Miss Knorr. I have felt drawn to you from the moment I met you. I can think of nobody I would prefer to talk with, to dance with, to simply be in a room with."

"Yet you have so often seemed so distant?"

Everton paused. The time had come to tell her the full truth. He so wanted to do it. He wanted her to know everything. Yet a part of him was afraid that she might turn away from him once she knew it all. He needed her. He loved her. He could not bear to lose her or be parted from her ever again. He knew that now. And so, there was so much more to lose than before. He glanced around the garden, trying to regulate his shallow, nervous breath.

"Are you quite well?" Miss Knorr asked him placing her delicate hand upon his arm. He took it between both his hands, marveling for a moment at the difference in size, and forced himself to smile at her.

"I am," he assured her. "But I have much to tell you. Perhaps we should take a seat somewhere, in full view of the house. I should not wish to ruin your reputation."

She chuckled at that. "I do not think it much matters, given I am too old and too poor to have a London Season. Young women such as myself do not fear the gossip and scandal of being caught alone in the gardens with a young man."

Everton laughed too. It was so like her to dismiss any concerns she might have for her own wellbeing. And he found it sad that she had such a low opinion of herself. "Nonsense, you are not too old," he insisted. "Mary was older when she was wed to William, as was Sophie when she met Wycliffe. And as to your lack of capital, well, that is not a concern to someone such as myself who will inherit a vast fortune someday."

Rather than looking reassured by his words, she actually looked more confused. Everton shook his head ruefully. "I am sorry, I am not explaining myself well. Please, can we go and sit on the terrace. I think I need a moment to get my thoughts together, so I might explain everything to you."

She nodded, happy to acquiesce. He offered her his arm and was delighted when she took it as they walked back towards the house. When they reached the terrace, he pulled out one of the cast iron chairs at the little table there for her, so she might sit, then took the seat opposite her. He pulled out the miniature and laid it on the table between them. She picked it up and studied it closely. "She looks so very like Caroline, but it is not her, is it?"

"No, it is not," Everton confirmed. "That is a portrait of my former fiancée, Katherine."

"Oh," Miss Knorr said. "I did not know you had been affianced."

"No, there are not many that would think to mention it now. It was many years ago." Everton expected her to ask him a hundred questions, but instead Miss Knorr sat patiently, waiting for him to say more. "We met when I was eighteen and she was sixteen. I believed her to be the love of my life. We had a long engagement, because of our age, and the plan was for us to be wed once I completed my education at Oxford." He paused, girding himself to say the next part out loud.

"She fell ill with influenza, a month or two before we were due to be married," he said quickly, spitting the words out before he could change his mind and stopper them back inside. "She was so very sick, and she got weaker and weaker and her fever never broke."

Miss Knorr reached out and placed her hands over his, where he had them clasped tightly, resting on the table in front of him. "Oh, Mr. Cormick, I am so terribly sorry. No wonder you have been so torn and troubled. Caroline's debut must have caused so many difficult memories to resurface for you."

"I must confess, the first time I saw her, I thought I was seeing a ghost."

"I am not surprised. The likeness is quite uncanny. All those times when you seemed a little distracted suddenly make perfect sense. You would sometimes stare at Caroline in such a way." She paused. "I think it lucky that Caroline is not the type to notice such things. She might have found it quite concerning otherwise."

"Oh, I had so hoped that nobody had noticed," Everton said. He had tried so hard to be discrete, and because Caroline had never mentioned it had assumed that his peculiar behavior had not been obvious to others. Usually, the subject of such scrutiny is fully aware of it, but Miss Knorr was right, it was not the sort of thing that Caroline would ever pay attention to. It simply hadn't mattered to her.

Miss Knorr sighed. "I think I understand why you were so out of sorts at the wedding now."

"You do?" he asked. "Because I did not, not for the longest time."

"It must have been a terrible experience for you, seeing Caroline as a bride. All those memories of what might have been with your Katherine."

"But I knew that Caroline was not Katherine. I had believed myself to be, finally, getting past my grief – yet it was as if a wave of memory engulfed me and wouldn't let me be."

"Grief is a strange thing. From day to day we can be managing quite well, content and happy, and then it floods over us once again," Miss Knorr said sagely. "My brother died when I was only fourteen. We had been so very close. And I grieved so hard for him when he was gone. It was part of the reason I did not really throw myself into my own Coming Out and therefore missed out on finding a husband. I was too broken-hearted and the young men of Devon and Cornwall did not wish for a maudlin bride."

"Is that why you were so keen to get away, to come to London? Because of your grief?" Everton asked. He had not known of Miss Knorr's brother. Such a loss, at such an early age must have been hard to bear.

"Partly," she admitted sadly. "I wished to get away from my shame, too, that I had not found a match."

They sat quietly. Everton pondered what she had said, the loss she had suffered. Yet she had never spoken of it to anyone, at least he did not think she had. She had certainly not ever spoken of it to him. And what was wrong with Society, that a young woman was left feeling ashamed, as if she was somehow at fault, if she did not find a husband by a certain age? It had always puzzled him, but now he was furious, on behalf of all the women who had been made to feel they weren't good enough or were somehow defective because they had failed to attract the attentions of some country squire who would probably have made their lives a misery anyway.

CHAPTER NINETEEN

Anne had not expected to talk of James. She never spoke of him. Her family had barely mentioned his name since Mama's spell of ill health. It was as if they could not bear to think of anything bad, for fear they might draw it closer. Anne had not even spoken to Mary about her beloved brother, though they had discussed so many things and had grown as close as sisters during her time in the Durand household.

Yet here she was, telling Mr. Cormick. She wanted him to know that she understood that grief could make you behave strangely, that she could easily forgive him – given the very strange position he had found himself in. It must have been quite disconcerting to see Caroline every time he turned around, and especially for her to then marry his younger brother. It was enough to make anyone act oddly.

"I am so very sorry," he said finally. "For my behavior – and for that of those ignorant fools during your Coming Out – and that you had to suffer such a painful loss."

"It is not easy to talk of. I don't think I've spoken of him in more than five years," Anne admitted.

"I rarely speak of her, too. Though she is always in my thoughts." He broke free of her hands and reached for the miniature. Anne had almost forgotten that she had been holding them, but she felt the loss of them like a dagger slicing through her skin, especially as he looked on the image with such love and stroked Katherine's cheek.

"Do you think it is ever possible to really get over someone, when you have loved so deeply?" Anne asked, curious as to what his reply might be. His answer could dash every faint hope that she had ever possessed, but she had to know.

"I do not think you ever stop loving someone, once you start," he said, setting down the portrait and looking into Anne's eyes deeply, as if he was searching for something only she might be able to give. "But I do believe that it is possible to let yourself love again – if you want it badly enough."

"And do you wish to love again?" Anne whispered, holding her breath as she waited for his answer. He did not answer immediately. Anne bit at her lip nervously.

"It is already too late for me," he said with a wry smile. Anne took a gulping breath. It wasn't the answer she had been hoping for, but it was probably the one she had expected.

"I am sorry," she said sadly. "I hope that one day you may change your mind."

He laughed and reached for her hands. "I do not mean it in that way," he said, shaking his head. "I meant that I already do love again, whether I thought it possible or not."

"You do?" Anne asked, her heart sinking. She had not seen him becoming particularly enamored with anyone throughout the Season, though he had always seemed thick as thieves with Lady Gertrude. But of course, Lady Gertrude. She would be a perfect match for a man such as Mr. Cormick. Why had Anne not seen it sooner? All those cozy chats the two of them had shared and the snatched moments in private away from even Miss Jessup.

Yet that did not entirely make sense, either. Both had insisted that their relationship was closer to that of siblings than anything else. And that was as it had always seemed. And when he had been disconcerted, at Henry's wedding over seeing Caroline, he had not ignored Lady Gertrude. He had danced with her and laughed with her as if nothing was different between them. No, it had been Anne, and only Anne that he had avoided. Could it possibly be that he had fallen in love with her? Such a thing seemed almost fantastical. It could not be true.

"Miss Knorr, I have struggled to understand my feelings in the past months," he said now. "And I know that has meant that my behavior has sometimes been more than a little erratic and strange. But that was simply because I was trying to wrestle – oftentimes most unsuccessfully – with my conscience." He paused and moved his chair closer to hers. Anne felt her breath catch once more.

"The more I saw of you," he went on, "the more we danced, the more we spoke, the more we shared, the more my feelings for you grew. I did not want to love anyone, ever again. I had vowed not to. I would not sully Katherine's memory by casting her aside. Yet those feelings would not be denied and I felt so terribly guilty – as if I was betraying her and the love we had shared. I simply did not know how to reconcile how I felt about you, with my love for her."

Anne could hardly believe what she was hearing. Had he truly just said that he had feelings for her? That she was the one that he had come to care for? She didn't dare speak. She hardly dared to breathe. Such a conversation as this one she was now sharing with Mr. Cormick had not even occurred in her wildest dreams – and he was so often in her dreams that she could hardly bear closing her eyes some nights.

"Miss Knorr, Anne – might I call you Anne?" he begged. She nodded, unable to find her voice. "I know I am not much of a man, that I still have much to learn and that there may be times when my grief at losing Katherine may sometimes still overwhelm me and make me unfit to be by your side, but I cannot imagine doing so any longer. I love you. I want you to be my wife – if you will have me?"

Anne had not ever expected to receive a proposal of marriage, much less one from a man she loved with all her heart. She wanted to say yes, she wanted to yell it, to let him know just how much she wanted exactly that – to be his bride. But she could not find her voice. Tears began to pour down her cheeks as she pinched herself, hard, to be sure she wasn't imagining this very unusual yet perfect moment. She nodded vigorously, hoping he would understand, would know she was saying yes, over and over again.

But it seemed that he did not. He got down on one knee, took her hands in his and pleaded with his eyes as he asked her again. "Please, Anne, please tell me? Will you marry me?"

"Yes, oh yes," she forced herself to whisper. He beamed and reached up to wipe the tears from her cheeks as he pressed a gentle kiss to her lips. Anne had never felt so alive, so vibrantly and completely alive as she did in that moment.

The sound of the door opening behind them did not alert them to Lady Mary emerging out into the gardens, to look for Anne. They were too lost in each other, right up until Mary moved closer and cleared her throat loudly. Anne giggled a little as they broke apart from their kiss. "I suppose we have no choice now, or there will be another scandal linked to your family name."

Mary gave her a blank look, but Mr. Cormick laughed loudly. "And we must not have that," he said. He turned to his hostess. "Lady Mary, I am so glad you have joined us. Miss Knorr finds herself in need of a chaperone, as I have just asked for her hand in marriage – and I do not think I can be trusted to keep my hands and lips to myself if we are not accompanied at all times."

Mary thankfully laughed, rather than being scandalized by his words. "Dearest Anne, I am so happy for you both," she said embracing Anne warmly, then kissing Mr. Cormick's cheek chastely. "And of course, I shall be delighted to act as a chaperone for you, as you did so beautifully for me. And with that in mind, I think it best if we all retire back inside. We are going to roll up the carpet in the library and dance. I know Anne will wish to join us."

Mr. Cormick escorted the two young women inside. "I think I had better tell my mother, before we mention this to anyone else – and I will travel with you to Devon, after the baptism, to ask for your father's permission," he assured Anne.

"There is no need, Mr. Cormick," Anne said bluntly, stopping them both in the corridor. She knew her father would say yes, as long as she was happy with the match. But she still felt that she needed to point out the one fact about her status they had not discussed, ever. "I shall write to him tomorrow and will tell him our intentions. There is no dowry to be arranged, and no inheritance you will gain so there is little that will need to be discussed. Is that a problem for you?"

Mr. Cormick simply smiled. "I have more than enough for that not to matter, my darling. And you really should call me Everton, don't you think?" With that, he pressed a chaste kiss to the top of her head and disappeared in search of his mother.

Anne pressed her fingers to her lips and smiled. Mary hugged her tightly. "I am so very happy for you," Mary said. "I know it is sometimes hard to believe, but this tiny little enclave of Society truly does not care for your past, or your inheritance. They may have to fight to get others to see it doesn't matter, from time to time, but every one of them knows that love is more important than money and status ever could be."

"It easy for them to feel that way, they all have both,"

Anne noted. "But I know you are right. None of them care for the so-called rules of etiquette – though they pay them lip-service when they must."

"I am so glad that you will be marrying Everton. Their estate in Hertfordshire is a day's carriage ride from here. We can visit one another often."

"I should like that, though I do hope that he will take me to their family hunting lodge in Scotland for our wedding tour. I so long to see the mountains there. I am told they are quite spectacular."

"I am sure he will be delighted to indulge you with something so easy for him to arrange," Mary said linking her arm with Anne's as they made their way along the corridor and into the library, where Lady Sophie and Lady Charlotte had already rolled back the rugs and had started organizing everyone into pairs ready for the first reel. Anne was delighted to have been partnered with Everton, though he was nowhere to be seen.

"Should we wait?" Lady Sophie said as Mrs. Watts took a seat at the pianoforte and began to play a lively tune.

"No, you go on ahead, "Anne said with a smile. "We have all the time in the world to join in when he returns."

Lady Sophie gave her a peculiar look, but quickly turned back to her husband and curtseyed deeply to him, as Mary did the same to Lord William and Lady Charlotte did to Captain Watts. The men then all bowed deeply, and the dance began. The reel was a little lopsided as the square was missing a fourth couple, but nobody minded that. Anne clapped in time to the music, along with Mr. Watts, the Duke of Compton and Mr.

Durand who had stopped talking business for a few moments at least.

The reel was almost done when Everton and his mother returned to the room. Mrs. Cormick was smiling, and she hurried straight to Anne's side and embraced her warmly. "Welcome to the family," she whispered, as Everton tapped on his glass to draw attention to himself and then directed a servant to hand out glasses of champagne to everyone present. Mrs. Watts stopped playing the pianoforte and the dancers turned to face him.

"I have great pleasure in announcing that I have just asked Miss Anne Knorr for her hand in marriage, and I am delighted to say that she has said yes," he said beaming from ear to ear.

Suddenly, Anne was surrounded by people, all hugging her and offering their congratulations. She had never felt so content, so accepted, so loved anywhere – other than back amongst her own family in Tulilly. Mrs. Cormick tapped on her glass, bringing the exuberant celebrations to a brief halt. "I cannot tell you how happy this news will make not just Everton and his bride, but every member of our family. Everyone here knows just how much his father and I worried for him, when he lost Katherine, but we are so very glad he has found Miss Knorr, to love and to love him." She raised her glass in a toast, which everyone joined in with enthusiastically and with genuine affection for them both. Anne struggled to swallow her champagne as she tried her best to hold back tears of joy.

EPILOGUE

Tulilly, January 1st, 1821

THE MANOR HOUSE was almost silent when Anne woke on the day of her wedding. She stretched and got out of bed, moving to the shutters and opening them and the windows wide so she could breathe in the fresh Devon air. There was a haze of mist hanging over the surrounding fields, but the sky was blue with only the barest handful of white clouds scudding across it. She smiled, still finding it hard to believe that this day had finally come.

Heather appeared at the head of the stable lads, who were carrying a large brass bath on their shoulders. They set it down in front of the fire, as Heather stoked the embers and added more wood to warm the room. The boys disappeared, and Heather proceeded to heat pot after pot of hot water on the fire, finally pouring them all into the tub so Anne might bathe. The young maid added rose petals and dried jasmine flowers before she left Anne to her privacy.

Anne pulled off her nightgown and slipped into the deep water. She felt the warmth seep into her muscles and bones, the scent of the flowers was intoxicating and relaxing. She could have stayed there all day, had the water stayed hot enough – and if she had not been about to marry the man she loved. As the clock struck nine, she quickly washed her body with a bar of soap Heather had left nearby and lathered her hair. A final dunk of her head under the water and she leapt out of the tub and grabbed a large bath sheet and wrapped it around herself.

Heather reappeared, as if she had perhaps been watching through the keyhole and began to pull an ivory comb through Anne's wet hair. She carefully began to pin it, so that it would dry in springy ringlets. If they did not set as they should, Heather would heat the tongs in the fire to ensure they would hold their shape for the entire day. Heather helped her into her undergarments and then disappeared.

A few minutes later, Mama entered Anne's room, carrying the gown that she had worn on the day she had married Papa. Anne smiled. It was a little old-fashioned, but the delicate lace and warm ivory satin had always been a part of her dream for this day. Mama laid it out carefully on the bed, so it would not crease or rumple, then hugged Anne tightly. "I am so proud of you, my darling," she said softly. "And I shall miss you. It has been so wonderful having you back home with us."

"Mama, Everton has promised me that we will visit

often. And his father has joined with Lord William's father and taken a share in the mines, so there will be lots of excuses for us to come."

"It is not the same," Mama said sadly. "When James died, I lost you both in some ways. You were never quite the same, and though you tried so hard to be what you thought we expected of you, I know how hard you struggled."

"I was so ashamed when I could not make a match," Anne admitted. "I never wanted to let you and Papa down, and I knew how much you needed me to marry well. I knew that the estate was not producing the yields it should and that Papa needed an injection of capital to turn it around. I hated that I could not make that happen for him."

"But we never expected you to bolster our situation by your marriage," her mother said, aghast at such a notion. "I am so sorry if you ever felt that was something we needed of you."

"It is what is expected of every young woman, is it not?" Anne said sadly.

"I suppose it is," Mama agreed. "But whether you intended it or not, you have managed to do so, and so far above any expectations we might have ever had. And we are so proud that Everton is the kind of man who does not mind one bit that you bring him nothing."

"I bring him love. It is all either of us wish from one another," Anne said a little dreamily.

"And that is a blessing that will help you to manage any hard times you face, but he has a fortune will ease your passage – and that is not to be dismissed," her mother warned her.

"I know," Anne said. "I have seen enough of being poor and the benefits of being rich to ever dismiss the need for enough capital to make your way in the world. I am glad that any children we may have will not have to struggle as we so often did."

"I missed so much time with you, when you were in London. I cannot quite believe what a poised and wise young woman you have become. James would be so proud of you."

"I miss him every day," Anne said quietly.

"Your father and I do, too."

They sat in contemplative silence for a few moments, then Mama stood up. "Now, let us get you dressed, so Heather can come back and finish your hair."

EVERTON STOOD at the end of the aisle of the Tulilly parish church, his brother, Henry, by his side. "You're sure you are ready for this?" Henry asked him.

"I have never been more sure of anything," Everton answered truthfully. He had not been spared moments of doubt in the past few days, but he was as sure as he could be that marrying Anne was precisely what he should be doing.

"And Katherine's ghost has finally been exorcised?" Henry's concern was touching. He so rarely ever noticed anyone or anything, that it was strange – but Everton was grateful for it.

"I think it has," he admitted.

"I'm so glad," Henry said with a cheeky grin. "You almost ruined our wedding when you saw Caroline walk up the aisle. I truly hope you don't come over all peculiar like that again."

"I am so sorry," Everton said, suddenly realizing that he had apologized to Anne, but not to Henry and his bride for his behavior on the day of their wedding. "It was like seeing her come back to life. I thought myself back then, waiting for her at the church." He paused. "I went there, you know, the day we should have been wed. I sat in the front pew, and I waited – as if she might come, like the lovesick fool I was."

"I knew," Henry said. "Mama sent me to watch over you. I didn't come in and kept out of sight when you came out. I think she wanted to be sure you didn't do anything stupid."

"Was I truly so bad?" Everton asked, surprised by what Henry had just said. He had believed he had kept the worst of his grief to himself, so as not to burden them. To find that they had known all along was disconcerting.

"You tried so hard to keep it all in. I think Mama feared it would eat you up inside, but you seemed to pull yourself together – though it wasn't until you met Miss Knorr that you really came alive again."

"I do wish someone had said some of this to me before," Everton mused.

"Would you have heard us out?" Henry asked him seriously. "You have always wanted to look after every-one, to protect all of us from our hurts – like talking with father so I might return to my studies. When you were hurt yourself, you simply put up a wall around your own pain so you could keep on doing that. Promise me, brother, that you won't do that again? That you will ask for help if you need it?"

"And people accuse you of not caring," Everton said, trying desperately to lighten the moment. Henry grinned.

"I care. I'm just not dramatic," he said simply. "Be happy with Miss Knorr. She is so very good for you."

At that moment, Everton could not respond to his brother, as the first chords of the wedding march sounded and Miss Knorr and her father, Sir John, appeared at the back of the church. She was dressed in a full-skirted ivory gown, covered with intricate lace. It nipped in at her waist, a style that had not been popular in many years, but one that showed off Anne's fine figure. She looked perfect. He could hardly take his eyes from her.

As Sir John placed her hand in his, Everton vowed silently and to nobody but himself, that he would love her and care for her with everything he was. She had changed him in every way. She had brought him back to himself, and he could never thank her enough for that. "I love you," he whispered, before the vicar began to speak.

"I love you," she said, smiling up at him, her rose-pink cheeks flushed with happiness.

The ceremony passed in a blur, all Everton could think of was the beauty of his bride and how lucky he was to have her in his life. Soon everyone present suddenly started cheering and he knew it was over. He was wed to the true love of his life. He offered her his arm and they made their way down the aisle, out into the bright sunshine. Everton dipped his head and kissed his wife's rosebud lips. "I don't deserve you, Mrs. Cormick," he said with a grin.

"No, it is I who does not deserve you, Mr. Cormick," she replied. "Mama reminded me today of how much I changed after James died. I got lost in my grief – and even though I tried not to speak of him or let him even enter my thoughts, he was there every minute of every day. Every man or boy I met was not ever good enough, because he was gone from my life. How could I ever consider replacing him."

"Yet, you fell in love with me?" Everton marveled. "A man as trapped by his grief as you were by yours."

"Perhaps that is why we found one another," Anne said. "We could understand each other. We knew the same pain, the same profound loss."

"The gaps by our side that could never be filled," Everton mused. "You may be right. But whatever it was that brought us together, whether it was our grief – or that we were simply finally ready to move on from it, I am glad of it. I will spend the rest of our lives together making you happy. I promise."

"And I will do the same," Anne echoed as he kissed her once more. "You are the love of my life. I know Katherine was yours, and I never expect to take her place in your heart."

"Darling Anne, always putting yourself last. You are the love of my life. I loved Katherine and always will – as you will always love your brother – but what I felt for her does not come close to what I feel for you. Know that, always. You are nobody's second choice – and especially not mine."

MY DEAR READER

Thank you for reading and supporting my books! I hope this story brought you some escape from the real world into the always captivating Regency world. A good story, especially one with a happy ending, just brightens your day and makes you feel good! If you enjoyed the book, would you leave a review on Amazon? Reviews are always appreciated.

Below is a complete list of all my books! Why not click and see if one of them can keep you entertained for a few hours?

Landon House

Mistaken for a Rake
A Selfish Heart
A Love Unbroken
A Christmas Match
A Most Suitable Bride
An Expectation of Love

Second Chance Regency Romance
Loving the Scarred Soldier
Second Chance for Love
A Family of her Own
A Spinster No More

Christmas Stories
Love and Christmas Wishes: Three Regency Romance
Novellas
A Family for Christmas
Mistletoe Magic: A Regency Romance
Home for Christmas Series Page

Happy Reading!
All my love,
Rose

A SNEAK PEAK OF LOVING
THE SCARRED SOLDIER

PROLOGUE

Caldor House, Alnerton, 1807

"I WILL GET YOU, Lady Charlotte Pierce," James whispered into her ear as he leaned just a smidge closer.

Charlotte looked over her shoulder to where Mrs. Crosby, her plump companion, was walking some feet behind them.

"Oh no you will not, James Watts, for I already have you," Charlotte replied cheekily, a playful grin on her face which exaggerated her dimples and the small cleft in her chin.

"Ah, but you only think that you have me. Truth be told, I have already laid claim to you these many years, but I allowed you to believe otherwise." He raised his chin slightly, the sun shining down on his handsome face. "There is no escaping it."

James folded his arms behind his back and Charlotte

peered up at him. James and her brother William were the same age, but James was minutely taller, with broader shoulders and a more relaxed air about him. William, unfortunately, was often far too austere – a characteristic for which he could thank their father, the Duke of Mormont.

Charlotte kept watching James in silence, waiting until he turned back in her direction. The moment he did, she grinned at him and promptly stuck out her tongue.

"You always like to best me James, but I tell you, one day, I will be the one who claims victory. Not you."

He grinned, his bright smile illuminating his oval face and gently sloping cheekbones.

"I look forward to it. You could win me over for the rest of my life," he whispered.

Charlotte's heart fluttered in her chest.

"You should not say such things, James," she replied. "Someone might think you mean what you say."

Her fingers rose to coil a tress of dark brown hair. She wrapped it around her index finger several times as she kept her eyes to the ground, waiting for his reply.

"You know I always mean what I say," he answered tersely.

Charlotte's feet faltered with her heart. What was he saying? Lately, James's conversations were more and more personal, much more than they ever had been before. They'd long had a closeness between them, ever since her former governess, Mrs. Northam, had married his father, John, who acted as the Duchy of Mormont's solicitor. Now, however, things were changing.

Slowly, she looked up at him again and was met by the intensity of his emerald eyes. It made her heart gallop. She could not maintain the connection and quickly looked away.

"James, do not toy with me."

"I would never toy with you about such things," he replied calmly.

Again, Charlotte's eyes could not refrain from looking at him. In recent years she had often found herself admiring the man he had become. He was no longer the boy she'd run after and played games with all those years ago. He was a man of twenty, two years her elder, and more esteemed in her sight than any of their acquaintances, save her brother.

Charlotte stopped walking when she realized that James had failed to follow. She turned to face him, perplexity filling her heart. These feelings were strange to her. She had no mother to teach her, and with Mrs. Northam, now Mrs. Watts, no longer in her family employ, she was left to decipher the world on her own, for her nurse, Mrs. Crosby, was not someone whom she felt she could ask about important matters.

"Charlotte."

The sound of her name on his lips was a cherished utterance. She was very fond of it, more than she ever dared to admit. They knew each other too well - what she felt could not be what she thought it was. Could it? When he looked at her the way he was doing now, she believed that it could be.

"We have known each other for what seems a life-time," James continued. The soft timbre of his voice was soothing. "We have played together and argued, cried, and laughed. We have seen each other in every... circumstance."

She laughed as the memory of their foray into his family's lakes, in nothing more than their undergarments as children suddenly flashed into her mind. Her father had been most upset by the indiscreet incident, which had left her soaked through, on the eve of a special dinner party. He had been equally displeased with the subsequent chill that had confined her to her bed. None of which had bothered her.

"We have."

James' brow furrowed slightly and she had the urge to smooth the wrinkles with her thumb. Customarily, she would have done so, but at that moment, with her feelings teetering on the brink, she dared not, lest they both fall over the edge.

Charlotte watched in curious fascination as the lump in James' throat bobbed up and down, and her dashing friend, ever confident, seemed to falter in his words. It was surprisingly endearing to see him so undone. She bit back a smile, but still felt the tug of it on her cheeks.

"You have to know... that is... you must be aware," James stuttered. His eyes were still lowered to his feet, but then, in a sudden burst of confidence, he forced himself to meet her gaze.

"Aware of what?" Charlotte questioned.

It took all of her strength to muster the words of the questions which curiosity demanded be answered. Did he feel as she did? Did his heart flutter at the sight of her as hers did whenever she saw him? Did he get cold, and his skin prickle when they touched? Was his head as full of her as hers was of him?

The more she thought of it, the more her emotions threatened to get the better of her. She quickly turned away, sure that her feelings were now evident on her face. She did not want to lose to him in this. She did not want to be the first to make her feelings known. In this one thing, she wanted to best him.

Charlotte's heart thundered in her ears. Her hands folded into defiant fists, as she determined not to be swayed by her emotions. She would be strong. She would let him speak and not give herself away, though she was aware that she may have already done so.

"Charlotte?" James' voice was a whisper. Then, she felt his hands settle gently on her arms. She was acutely aware of the proximity of his body to hers. This was not their normal interaction. Yes, they were close, had even embraced, but the feelings which filled her at that moment were far greater, more powerful – consuming. Her stomach felt as if it would take flight. "You feel it too, don't you?" he continued to whisper.

"Feel what?" Charlotte replied as her voice shook.

She glanced in the direction of Mrs. Crosby. The woman was pretending to look at the leaves on one of the potted plants, but glances in their direction made Charlotte aware that she was keeping a close eye on them, in case things went too far.

"She will not come. I asked her not to."

Charlotte's eyes widened and her breath caught in her throat at James' confession.

"You did what?"

"I asked Mrs. Crosby to give us a moment of privacy," he continued. "There is something very particular which I wish to say to you, Charlotte. Something best said to your face and not your back."

She could hear the slight lilt of laughter in his voice, but also nervousness.

"James," she replied. "You can tell me anything. You always have."

Her words were answered with a gentle tug on her arms, turning her to face him. She did not resist. She could not. All strength was gone from her limbs and she was at the mercy of her feelings, which would not be hidden.

Their eyes met and Charlotte thought she might faint. Her head felt light, her heart was gone, only large butterfly wings remained, beating frantically in her chest, as smaller ones filled her belly. What was happening?

He did not remove his hands from her arms, Instead, he stepped closer, and Charlotte felt sure that the world had stopped and she no longer remembered how to breathe.

"You and William have always been my dearest friends," James stated. "But you, Charlotte, you have become something infinitely more dear to me." Warmth washed up her neck and she was sure that her cheeks were now painted in crimson. Yet she could not speak. "I know that you have only ever considered me as a friend, and for a long time, I had accepted that fact. I thought I could live with it, but I cannot. I cannot be content with simply being your friend when I desire to be something much more."

Charlotte raised a hand and placed it on his chest to stop him, but the beating beneath her fingers caused her to pause. His heart was racing just like hers.

James looked at her delicate fingers and then placed his hand over hers, holding it over his heart.

"This is what I feel every time I am near you. I cannot stop it. I have tried, but nothing works. I think it is because I do not wish it to. I like that you do this to me. You are the only one who can."

Her breathing erratic, Charlotte tried to think. She knew all the proper things to do, the decorum that was required, but how did one have such decorum with someone who had nursed your wounds and wiped your tears, often after having been responsible for causing them? One who knew you better than anyone else did?

"I know there are many who desire you," James continued. "I am not so foolish as to believe that I am the only one who cares for you, but I would hope I might have some advantage over those others."

"Of whom do you speak? I know of no one," Charlotte questioned, bewildered.

His emerald eyes were ablaze.

"Do you mean to tell me that there is no other who wishes your hand?"

Charlotte's hearing became hollow, only the sound of what seemed to be rushing water could be heard as the words left his lips. She was eighteen. She had never had anyone desire her hand, at least not that she knew of. Such matters were for her father, and none dared speak to her before presenting their proposal to him. None but James, that is. He was allowed certain liberties that other gentlemen were not, being such a close family friend.

"What are you saying?" she whispered, "Be plain."

He smiled at her.

"Always so straightforward."

"Always skirting around the subject," she replied. "Just tell me. Do not keep me on tenterhooks." She squeezed his hand lightly. "I want to hear the words."

James stepped closer, the space between them almost entirely gone as he lowered his head to her ear and whispered.

"I love you, Charlotte. I have always loved you."

The smile his words elicited could not be contained, and as their eyes met, she answered him.

"I love you, too, James. I always have."

$\sim$

CALDOR HOUSE, Alnerton, 1809

"LADY CHARLOTTE. LADY CHARLOTTE." A soft voice repeated her name, but Charlotte was doing her utmost to resist. "You must rouse yourself, Lady Charlotte. The day is already upon us and you must get ready."

It was Sophie Lefebvre, her new companion. Her father had finally been swayed to Charlotte's view that Mrs. Crosby was no longer suitable and that a woman closer to her age would be a far better choice. Sophie, who was also almost twenty, the daughter of an English-woman and a Frenchman, her family in exile from

France as a result of the war, had seemed a good choice to replace Mrs. Crosby.

Charlotte forced her dark brown eyes open. The room was still mostly in darkness, but Sophie had the chambermaids already at work opening the blinds, while she set about laying out Charlotte's attire in readiness.

"Please, Lady Charlotte. You do not want to keep your brother and the duke waiting. It would be disrespectful to Monsieur Watts if you were to arrive late," Sophie pleaded. "You would not want to do that."

Sophie knew those words would force Charlotte from her bed, though no words could change how Charlotte felt, not on that day.

Charlotte forced herself to rise from her four-poster bed, then padded to the window, her bare feet making no noise as she crossed the room. She looked out to where grey mists covered the gardens. The sky was overcast and the sun was completely hidden. It was as if the day shared her feelings.

"Quickly, Lady Charlotte," Sophie continued. She came to stand beside Charlotte. "I know that you do not wish to go, but you must."

"Must I?" Charlotte retorted weakly. "It will change nothing."

Sophie sighed.

"No, it will not. It is not supposed to. It is for you to show the respect which Monsieur Watts deserves. Please, come from the window and let me help you dress."

Charlotte was a doll in Sophie's hands. She turned her and twisted her, made her sit, and stand, all while Charlotte uttered not a word. Finally, once her shoes were on and her black dress laced and every adornment in place, she sat her before the mirror.

The young woman who looked back at her was foreign to her eyes. Her skin was far paler than it used to be. Her eyes less bright and her long dark brown hair seemed a dull greyish-black. Everything seemed to be cast in shades of grey.

The white collar which rose around her neck itched, but Charlotte cared little about it. It was the only contrast to the black of the rest of her ensemble. Once her hair was curled and pinned, Sophie placed a black feathered cap on her head.

"C'est fini! You are done!"

Charlotte didn't reply. Instead, she stood and strode out of her chamber.

She found William loitering in the hall, waiting for her. Her brother was not himself either, as was evident from the solemn expression on his face. He walked toward her and took her hand, hooking it gently over his arm.

"How are you this morning, Charlotte? We missed you at breakfast."

"How should I be?" she answered absently.

Her eyes glanced over the balcony to the floor below.

"It was a foolish question," William replied. "Forgive me. I do not know how to deal with these matters."

She turned to her brother.

"Save Mother, we are unaccustomed to such things. You are forgiven."

He smiled at her before proceeding, in silence, to escort her down the stairs and out the door, to where the carriage waited for them. It was decorated appropriately; pulled by matched black horses with black plumes upon their heads. The driver was similarly dressed in black and the carriage was of the same color.

Charlotte's feet faltered, but William bore her up and helped her inside. Their father was already waiting.

"That took you too long," he commented harshly. "It isn't right to be late for such things. It is gross disrespect, Charlotte. You should know better. Both of you."

"Forgive me, Father," William replied. "It was my fault entirely."

"All the worse. You, being the elder, should direct your sister appropriately, and not pander to such poor conduct. See to it that it never happens again."

"Of course, Father. Never again," William replied.

Charlotte remained silent, and as the carriage moved forward, her gaze stayed fixed out the window.

She recognized none of the landscape as they passed, her mind too full to allow her to truly see what was before her, and she shunned the sight of Watton Hall, James' former home. She could not look upon it without losing her composure. She chose to close her eyes until she was sure they were well past it. The next sight she saw, consequently, was that of Alnerton Village Church.

The chapel was overflowing with mourners, but a special place had been reserved for them, and William helped her to it. Charlotte sat in silence, refusing to look at the empty coffin at the front of the church.

James was not there. His body had been lost somewhere in Roliça, Portugal, where he'd fallen during the battle with the French the year before. It had taken months for them to get news of his death, and more still for his father to come to terms with it, enough to have the memorial service held.

They all struggled to believe it – Captain James Watts, a fine young man, his father's pride and joy, an adoring stepson and caring and devoted friend, and the man Charlotte loved, was dead.

The Reverend Moore said a great many things about James, but they were only shadows of the truth. James was far more than the vicar claimed. The vicar hadn't known James as she did.

She could have told them of the man he truly was, the gentle soul who'd tended her knee when she fell among the brambles. The man who'd taken every opportunity to touch her hand whenever he could, and who had loved to make her laugh.

The man whose face she still saw every time she closed her eyes.

Once the rites were performed, Charlotte and her family gathered with Mr and Mrs Watts to bury the son they'd lost.

She was coping, in control, until the moment the pallbearers brought the coffin to the grave. Then, Charlotte lost all semblance of calm.

The tears flowed from her eyes and her body was wracked with uncontrollable spasms. She gasped for breath but found none. She was suffocating where she stood. The air she struggled to breathe was gone. James was gone.

William did his best to console her, but there was no consolation for her grief - it was a physical pain she could not bear, and she crumbled under the weight of it. Seconds later, her brother's strong arms were carrying her away from the sight, away from sympathetic, pitying eyes, to the safety of their carriage. Their father followed close behind, and soon they were on their way home.

Charlotte had no recollection of the return journey. Her room was dark when she awoke, much later, and she was still dressed in her mourning gown. Her feathered cap was gone.

She rolled onto her back but no sooner had she done so than fresh tears rolled down her cheeks. He was gone. James was never coming back.

It was heartbreak like no other. She had been a child, barely two, when her mother had passed away, and she had no true recollection of that loss. James, though, was different. She had known him. She had cared for him. She had loved him.

Silent tears kept her company as she lay in the dark until her eyes could weep no more. Then, Charlotte forced herself to sit up. The gloom of her room was oppressive - she needed to escape it, she needed light to help her fight the darkness which threatened to overtake her. She rushed to her chamber door, forgetting to don stockings or shoes, and simply walked along the corridor with no plan of where she was going.

Soon, she heard her father's voice. She followed it until she stood outside his office. She listened; he was in conversation with someone - her brother William she was sure - and she heard her name mentioned.

"The Marquess of Dornthorpe?" her brother asked.

"Yes. He has written to propose his interest in an

alliance between our families. He is seeking your sister's hand for his son, Malcolm, Earl of Benton."

"Father, it is too soon to present such a proposal to Charlotte. She is still mourning for James."

"She will recover. Such an alliance should be most agreeable to all parties. However, I note your point. I will give her a few weeks to mourn his loss before informing her of the betrothal."

"Betrothal? Father, don't you think it prudent to ask Charlotte if she has any interest in the man before arranging an engagement. She has met him but four times, if I remember right. And a betrothal during mourning – that will set the gossips' tongues wagging."

"Four times was more than enough for your mother to decide to marry me. I do not see why your sister should be any different. As for the gossips – well, technically, James is no relation of ours, and so mourning is not a requirement."

"Father, please..."

"I have made my decision, William. Your sister will marry Malcolm Tate, and become the Countess of Benton, and eventually the Marchioness of Dornthorpe. Our family will sit on two seats, Dornthorpe and Mormont. Such a fortunate alliance is to be envied indeed."

Her knees gave out and the floor rushed up, as Charlotte slumped against the wall. That was it? James was barely in his grave and yet she was given to another? It was at that moment that she realized how conniving her father truly was. He cared nothing for her pain and hurt, only for their family's good standing.

Charlotte had no strength to remove herself from outside the door. *Let them find me here,* she thought. *Let them know that I am aware of what they had discussed without her. Let them see what it has done to me. Maybe that would touch father's heart.*

She might hope so, but she suspected it was unlikely.

CHAPTER ONE

C aldor House, Alnerton, 1814

CHARLOTTE LOOKED up at the imposing building toward which they were driving. Caldor House was still the same, all these years later, and as it had in the past, it filled her heart with heaviness. The only reason she was returning to her father's home was for the sake of her son. George needed a male influence, and without his father, he had only her father and William to guide him, for her late husband's father now had suffered a debilitating illness.

She looked over to where her sleeping child lay. He was so much like Malcolm that it made her smile to think of it. She stroked his hair gently. She had not loved Malcolm when she'd married him, but he was the escape she'd needed – from grief and from loneliness.

In return, she had given him the gift of their son – the

son he had hoped for, to carry on his family name. She was happy that she'd been able to do so before his time on earth was over. Her only regret was that he would not be there to see George grow into a man he would be proud of.

The carriage stopped on the broad expanse of gravel in front of the house. The door opened, and there, standing in his usual fine attire, was her brother William. A broad smile spread across his face as he immediately took the stairs at a rapid pace to come toward her.

"Charlotte!" he called.

She smiled in return as the coachman opened the door for her and helped her down.

"William, how wonderful to see you."

She wrapped her arms around him. It felt like a lifetime since they had last seen each other, and she had missed him dearly - it was his presence here, more than anything, which had brought her back to her childhood home.

"How was your journey?" William asked.

"Long and tiring. George is asleep in the carriage," Charlotte replied.

"Then I shall gather him up and carry him into the house."

William strode toward the carriage and, moments later, cradled her son in his arms. George looked angelic, nestled against his uncle's chest, completely safe from all harm.

It wasn't easy being alone and so far from home. Once Malcolm had died, everything had changed. Suddenly the security Charlotte knew no longer existed.

There was also the threat from those who wished to take from her son what was rightfully his, the title of Earl of Benton, and, likely quite soon, that of Marquess of Dorn-thorpe, when his ailing grandfather died. He was too young, but he would learn under her father, and when he was old enough, he would return and take his place. In the meantime, Malcolm's trusted steward, Mr. Charlesworth, was tending to matters and would send Charlotte regular reports.

"He weighs nothing," William commented as they walked up the stairs.

"To you perhaps, but to me, he weighs little less than a ton," Charlotte mused. "Is Father at home?"

William's expression fell.

"He had to remain in town to see to some pressing matters with our bankers. I have only just returned myself. I wanted to be here for your arrival. Father will return by tea time."

Charlotte nodded in understanding - it was for the best that her father was not present. It gave her time to settle herself, to some extent, before seeing him again. Since her marriage, Charlotte had seen little of her father. He had stayed in Alnerton or at their townhouse in London and found no reason to visit her, not even at the birth of his grandson, although he had sent a card and an expensive gift.

"I have prepared your old rooms for you and converted the adjoining suite into a nursery for George. I thought it best to keep him near you. He will be unfa-miliar with these surroundings for a time."

Charlotte smiled.

"Thank you, William. You think of everything."

"I try to," he replied with a grin. "Especially when it comes to matters of my sister and nephew."

They were greeted at the door by almost all of the household staff, their smiling faces bright as they welcomed her back. Charlotte was slightly overwhelmed. She'd almost forgotten them, for she had put Caldor House behind her on the day she'd left, thinking she would never return to it. Unfortunately, fate had other plans for her, and here she was.

Once the welcome was over, she followed William upstairs as footmen scurried to unload all of her possessions and carry the steamer trunks up to her rooms. William carried George into the nursery and settled him into bed without him even waking. Leaving a nursemaid watching over him as he slept, William opened the door and ushered her through into her rooms.

The space was bright, the curtains pulled wide to allow the sun into the room, but the memories lingered there. She could remember the last night she'd spent in that room, and the many before that, filled with hopes, fears, and then abiding grief.

I thought never to see this room again, yet, here I am.

"Is everything to your liking?" William said from behind her.

Charlotte turned to him, slowly untying the ribbon from beneath her chin as she removed her bonnet.

"Everything is just as I remember it."

"I wanted it to be as easy an adjustment for you as possible."

He smiled at her.

"I missed you very much," Charlotte replied.

Sadness began to prick her eyes with tears.

"And I, you," William replied as she strode toward him.

She fell into her brother's embrace and held him tightly as memories overwhelmed her. His hand gently patted her back as he spoke soothingly in her ear.

"I know it has been frightfully difficult for you, Charlotte. I wish I could have made it better. A thousand times I have wished I could have changed the things that happened, but I hope you know I had no control over those circumstances."

"Hush," Charlotte urged. "Do not speak of it. I know what you would have done if you could." She looked up at him. "Now, leave me alone for a while. I shall rest before tea."

"Of course."

William nodded and excused himself.

She lay back on the bed intending to rest, but her mind resisted that intent. Memories tumbled through her mind, leaving her wide awake and out of sorts. She lay on her bed, her hands clasped over her stomach as she looked up at the canopy above her, until the exhaustion from the long day of travel, and all that had gone before, caught up with her, and sleep overtook her.

It was nearly teatime when Charlotte awoke. Immediately, she worried about George, but when she called for the maid, she was assured that George had eaten his meal, had looked in to see his mother sleeping, and had happily gone back into the nursery with the maid, to play with his toys.

Charlotte allowed the maid to dress her in a gown suitable for dining with her father. Her father kept an elegant table at all times and expected everyone to conform to his expectations.

Her dress was mint green in color, made from the finest silk and lace. It had been a gift from Malcolm before he became ill. Charlotte was glad that, now her mourning was done, she could wear colors again. The year of mourning had taken a toll on her, shut away at Bentonmere Park, but it had also been peaceful. Now, for George's sake, it was time to be visible to the world again.

She smoothed her hands over her stomach as she looked at her reflection in the mirror. Her shape had changed after having George. She no longer had a girl's figure, but it was a pleasing figure nonetheless. She twisted a curl of dark hair around her finger then pushed it back into place before turning away.

The dining room was set when Charlotte arrived. William lingered by the door waiting for her.

"Father isn't here as yet," he informed her.

"Shall we sit then and wait?"

"We may as well. You know how he is about punctuality, even if he is not so himself," her brother answered with a light laugh.

He hooked his arm and held it out to her.

Charlotte allowed her brother his little trifles of amusement. He'd had so little of humor in his youth, for he'd lived under their father's thumb, ever aware that he was to inherit his title and position, as Duke, and also his vast portfolio of investments, in banking and shipping. It had always been a heavy burden for William to bear, and because of that, Charlotte hardly ever allowed herself the luxury of sharing her burdens with her brother.

James had always been the person she'd shared such things with.

The thought of her former love gave her a moment of pause. It always did. Despite his death, James Watts had really never left her, even throughout her marriage, he was, in a way, ever-present. He was still a comfort to her in her thoughts, even if he was no longer in the world.

"How are Father's affairs?" she questioned once they were seated.

William sighed.

"When it comes to matters pertaining to the smooth running of the Duchy, it is never a straightforward task. Father insists upon seeing to every detail, no matter how small. He leaves me little responsibility – though he expects me to pay as close attention as he does himself."

She looked at him with concern. He was clearly frustrated at the lack of trust their father was showing him.

"Do you like it at all? Working with Father, I mean?"

"There are days when I love it. Learning about all the elements involved in the Duchy's management, from managing the rents to investing the proceeds from the land well – it is absorbing and challenging. Many in Father's place would entrust such work to managers and bailiffs – but he prides himself that it is a matter of honor."

"Has there been some cause for a loss?"

Charlotte shook her head lightly. Her brother was a clever man. He had left Cambridge with high praise from his tutors, and he was not one to shirk his duties. But

Father was very demanding. It could only be hard on William to have to always listen and never be permitted to give his opinion or have any autonomy.

They were sipping wine and talking when their father finally arrived. He marched into the room without care or apology and promptly seated himself at the head of the table.

"Charlotte," he stated. "I am glad to see that you that have arrived and remembered how I prefer to go on here."

"Thank you, Father."

"Where is the boy?"

"George is with Mrs. White, his nurse. He will be in bed by now."

"Good, a boy needs routine and order - structure makes a man," her father continued. He picked up the small bell which sat to his right and rang it, as an indication to the staff to serve dinner.

The meal was delicious - four courses as usual - including dessert. Her father always insisted upon it, although why she never knew. It was simply the way it was.

"How is Mrs. Watts, William? Has she improved at all?" her father asked through a mouthful of the roast.

"I'm afraid not, Father. Mr Watts told me only yesterday that she has taken a turn for the worse."

"Unfortunate. We are sure to have a funeral to attend soon," her father continued.

Charlotte dropped her knife in alarm.

"Funeral? Is Mrs. Watts so ill?"

"I am afraid so," William explained. "It has been

several months now since she first became ill and there seems to be no end in sight. I am sorry to have to tell you this on your first day back."

She could hardly think. Beatrice Watts was the only mother figure Charlotte had ever known. The thought of her death was unbearable. How would her husband take that news after already having lost James?

"I will go to see her tomorrow," Charlotte blurted.

It was her father's turn to drop his cutlery. However, he recovered quickly and carried on as if nothing had happened.

"I do not think that is wise, Charlotte. Mrs. Watts is very ill and you have a child to consider. You cannot allow yourself to be so exposed."

"What exposure can there be, Father? I will take the customary precautions. I am sure that you and William have visited her, and neither of you has become ill."

"I think Father is correct, Charlotte. You have only just returned here, perhaps you should allow yourself some time to adjust before visiting the Watts," William agreed.

She looked at him perplexed.

"William, Mrs. Watts has tended to us our entire lives. How can I be so unfair as to avoid her, especially under these circumstances? I cannot. I will not. I shall visit her tomorrow."

The subject died immediately, but Charlotte did not miss the silent exchange between her brother and father, an exchange of looks which puzzled her completely. She did not understand their thinking but she would not be persuaded by it. Mrs. Watts was a lovely woman and she would see her, and care for her if it would give her any comfort at all.

After tea, Charlotte retreated to the parlor, but she was not alone for long. Mrs. White brought George to her soon after, the young child having woken fretful and calling for her. She set her son on the floor with his blocks and joined him.

"A little of this and you will be tired again in no time, won't you George?" she said as she placed one block on top of the other. George hit the floor with his.

They continued like that for several minutes before they were joined by William. Her brother watched them with a silent grin as they played. His presence was comforting and Charlotte was happy to have him there and thankful that their father was absent.

"I am sorry I could not stay long after the funeral," William said suddenly.

Charlotte looked at him perplexed.

"Why do you bring it up?"

"I do not think I have apologized enough for it. You needed me after his passing and I could not be there for you as I should."

"William, you had pressing work. I understood," Charlotte assured him.

William had only stayed a fortnight after Malcolm was laid to rest. Charlotte had wanted him to stay longer, but the management of the estates and the investments had called him away, and she could not bring herself to ask him to prolong his stay regardless. She held no grudge toward him for it. It was the way of the world, and her loss was no large factor in his life, only hers.

"Thank you, Charlotte. You have always been too kind in everything," William continued. "Do you still intend to visit Mrs. Watts tomorrow?"

"Of course," she replied. "I said I would and I shall do so. I shall make arrangements in the morning to visit her during the afternoon."

William was silent for a moment. Charlotte could see he was contemplating something, more than likely the bank, or next year's crop plantings on one of the estates – he never stopped thinking of such things, it seemed to her.

"Will you excuse me, Charlotte? I have a matter I must urgently attend to."

"Of course."

William came to them and ruffled George's hair before leaving the room. Charlotte remained with her son, playing with his blocks until his eyes grew heavy again, and he curled beside her on the floor to sleep.

She lifted George and carried him from the room, leaving the blocks where they lay, holding his head gently against her shoulder as she walked toward the stairs and their rooms. On her way up, she happened to turn, and glance down, to see William giving a letter to a footman, who immediately left the house. Her brow furrowed. Who was William writing to at such an hour?

THERE IS a huge secret that Lady Charlotte discovers and it will change her life! Check out the rest of the story in the Kindle Store Loving the Scarred Soldier

JOIN MY MAILING LIST

Sign up for my newsletter to stay up to date on new releases, contests, giveaways, freebies, and deals!

Free book with signup!

Monthly Facebook Giveaways! Books and Amazon gift cards!
Join me on Facebook: https://www.
facebook.com/rosepearsonauthor

Website: www.RosePearsonAuthor.com

Follow me on Goodreads: Author Page

You can also follow me on Bookbub!
Click on the picture below – see the Follow button?

Made in the USA
Middletown, DE
15 October 2021